MASTER
CLASS

FIRST THREE LESSONS

paige press

MASTER CLASS

FIRST THREE LESSONS

RAVEN JAYNE

Paige Press
Leander, TX 78641

Ebook:
ISBN: 978-1-953520-49-4

Print:
ISBN: 978-1-953520-50-0

ALSO BY RAVEN JAYNE

ABOUT THIS BOOK

Ten lessons are all that stand between me and my future...
My entire life has been determined for me.
I will be the trophy wife of a powerful man.
But another powerful man stands between us.
The first lesson he teaches me is obedience.
The second, patience.
My third lesson is supposed to be learning to control my mind.
But maybe I'd prefer he do it for me...

OBEY

_____

A master's class in surrender.

My entire life, I was trained to be a perfect bride.
I thought I was ready for my wedding.
I longed to meet the man who would be my husband.
Instead I met *him*—
The Master.
He says I'm not good enough.
He says I haven't learned everything I need.
Ten lessons are all that stand between me and my future.
But the sensual journey he takes me on will teach me more
than I ever dreamed.

1

———

THWACK. Thwack. Thwack.

The envelope is fancy, made of thick, heavy paper, and so is the letter inside; every time my father slaps them against the heel of his hand, the sound echoes faintly.

I stand behind him, my body held at attention, as he stares over the prow of our yacht—*The Salty Baby*. We've been tied up in harbor for a few hours—just long enough for the mail to come in. I don't know what the letter says, or who it's from; I don't know whether those *thwack*s mean he's angry, or just lost in thought. All I know is that my companion, Jane, came and got me from my room, and told me to go to my father, and so here I am. I was born and raised to be an obedient daughter, and I enjoy being good at what I do, which is everything a traditional school would have taught me, and so much more.

A shaft of late-afternoon sunlight creeps across the yacht's teak flooring, warming my bare feet and making my fresh pedicure glisten, the faint hints of iridescence in the pink polish glimmering like tiny disco balls. My legs are bare underneath my new sundress, a piece from Dior's resort collection that was delivered to the boat by helicopter, shipped to us as soon as it came off the runway. The skirt is light and fluttery, dancing in the breeze, and I have to focus to keep myself from smoothing it down every ten seconds. My hands must remain calm and at my sides. I do not want to be seen fidgeting like a child.

My patience is rewarded when my father turns around and finds me in first position, face placid and expectant, exactly as I ought to be.

"Your husband," he says, "has sent you a gift." He *thwacks* the letter against his palm one more time, for emphasis. "A lovely piece of property in the Maldives, for your very own."

A smile blossoms on my face. I've never met this man— technically, he isn't my husband yet, but I've been promised to him for as long as I can remember. I've always wondered what he would be like, and what our life together would be like. This seems like an excellent start. I'm already planning what to pack—my pink Eres bikini, and the new Missoni one, plus a Pucci coverup or two—so I'm distracted when I respond, too excited to play anything cool. "That's... Will he take me there? Will I finally meet him?"

My father seems less enthused. "I can't say yet," he informs me, slipping the envelope into his pocket. I haven't even caught a glimpse of my husband's handwriting—any crumb or clue that might give me a sense of him beyond what I already know: that his family is like mine. That our families' positions will be strengthened by our union. That he's waited his whole life for me, too.

I am not just a Newmont, but the only daughter of William Newmont. You probably haven't heard of us, but don't worry. Most haven't. We're richer than most people can understand, and more secretive than anyone outside our circles can imagine. And in our circles, alliances are worth millions. Sometimes—often—even more.

Of course, the best way to cement an alliance is marriage. And so my marriage is, in a sense, the family business.

It's strange to think that soon I'll meet the man who has shaped my entire life without ever touching it directly. My husband has been my carrot and my stick since I was a child: through private tutoring, through dance lessons, through violin practice and coding tests and horseback riding, and the endless hours spent learning my colors and angles and contouring and hairstyles. Every moment of my life has been devoted to creating the perfect wife for him, whoever he might be, and whatever he might want.

So I can't help testing my father's resolve, just a little, even though I know it's likely foolish. William Newmont isn't a man who tells you anything more than he wants to. "You can't tell me who he is? Even now?"

"You'll see him every day for the rest of your life soon enough," Daddy says. "In the meantime, your focus needs to be on your continued education, not mooning around."

Of course he's right, and I know it. But for all of my carefully held exterior, inside, I'm simmering with impatience. My twenty-first birthday was two full weeks ago; I had thought that by now I'd be planning an engagement party, picking out my own envelopes and stationery, not staring longingly at the hidden contents of someone else's. I've been training my whole life; this was supposed to be the year I stopped learning and started doing. So I feel like I've earned a little mooning, even if my father doesn't agree.

I realize that he hasn't moved from where he's standing, still regarding me thoughtfully, and I snap back to attention. This conversation isn't over yet, apparently.

"The gift has strings," he says.

I nod graciously, stifling a laugh. What present doesn't? I've spent my whole life earning access to my family's unimaginable wealth and influence one way or another. I've groomed myself to please like a Persian cat. I don't have much experience in the wider world, but I know ours intimately, and I've never been given something I didn't have to pay something for in return. "What are they?" I ask.

"He wants you to have some additional training."

"But...what is there I haven't studied?" If he's worried about me in the Maldives, I've been SCUBA certified since I was fourteen. What more must I learn that he can't teach me himself?

My father has had enough of my impertinence for one day. "Because your *husband* requested it, and your *father* agreed," he says. "He hired an agency to manage your finishing. You will meet your mentor tomorrow at his office. Jane will be advised of the place and time."

He isn't the only one who can lose his temper. And as long as I'm still a child, unmarried and in her family home, I'm going to act like one. I stamp my foot and roll my eyes. "I hate this! Why can't you just tell him no?"

"And why would I do that? You've spent your entire life waiting for this. What's a little bit longer?"

That depends heavily on what exactly "a little bit longer" means. I know plenty about patience but I'm tired of exercising it. "How long will it take?"

"As long as it does." My father flips his sunglasses up onto his head, and at last I see his eyes, which are blue like mine. There's a challenge in them now, half expectation and half taunt, which makes my blood sing in my veins. "Come on, princess," he says. "You're good at everything. This will be easy."

I duck my face to hide my smile. I don't want to come off smug, but he's not wrong. Like I said, I've been tutored in everything under the sun my whole life, and not only am I an excellent student when I set my mind to it, there isn't much I can't pick up on the fly. Maybe if I devote a little extra time to this, study super hard, I'll be able to fly through it in a week or two, and then get on with the rest of my life. Maybe I can even get started now, so when I show up to training tomorrow, I won't be caught flat-footed. "What kind of finishing?" I ask.

Daddy's phone rings. He looks at it. I can't tell what's in his eyes now, but his voice is uninflected, even, bored, almost. "Erotic," he says.

Then he lifts the phone to his ear and walks away to take the call.

Once he's wandered down the stairs to one of the lower decks, I allow myself to sink into a puddle of frustration on the floor, the raw silk of my skirt poufing up around me like dandelion floss. I spent the first twenty-one years of my life learning to be everything a man might want in a wife; I pushed myself to be the best at everything I did because I knew there was a time limit on it, a day when I could stop practicing and start actually living.

I've never touched a man before—not intimately, anyway —but I always assumed that my husband would teach me what he wanted in bed himself. I'm a quick study, and I've certainly thought about it enough. If that's where his mind is, then I don't understand why he wants me in another series of classrooms instead of in his bed already.

But I don't understand so many of the decisions men make. Hopefully I will soon.

Like Daddy said, I'll just have to wait a little bit longer, is all.

———

I HAVE to give my husband this: he does not skimp on instructions.

When I arrive back at the compound that afternoon, to

the guesthouse on the Newmont estate by the coast, there's a note waiting for me that specifies not just where to be (an address on one of the fanciest streets in the business district) and when (basically as soon as the sun comes up tomorrow morning), but also what to wear to my appointment, down to my shoes and underwear.

I have to rush out again as I read the list, since I don't have any of the things he wants; Jane calls ahead for me, and by the time I arrive at the boutique, they've tracked down the blue and gray Alaïa sweater dress and the black patent leather Christian Louboutin heels he's requested. The lingerie is a bit easier, since they already have my measurements at Agent Provocateur, so I pick that up last.

When I walk into the store, my favorite salesgirl, Monica, is waiting for me with a ribbon-topped bag and a sly smile. "Who's this for?" she asks. "I've never seen you pick out anything like this for yourself."

I peek inside the bag. My husband's instructions were very specific: he wanted me in a matching set of bra and panties, black silk dotted with appliqued daises, a look that's both sexier and more innocent than the solid-colored silks I usually go for. I'm already fantasizing about putting it on tomorrow, his first real gift to me sliding between my legs and cupping my breasts under my clothes. My pussy pulses a little bit at the thought.

I want to meet him as soon as possible, but the intrigue of all of this is a little bit sexy, too.

The feeling of anticipation builds up, and I come home with heavy bags and my heart hammering in my chest. I've worn hundreds of beautiful things in my life; my father has picked out my outfits on some occasions, and I spent several years under the tutelage of a French stylist who dressed me up like her doll whenever she wanted.

But there's something different about this, I think, as I

finger the red satin ribbon Monica tied around the box with tomorrow's underwear in them. My husband went to some trouble to pick out what he thought would look good on me; this will be my first chance to demonstrate my desirability to him, and it thrills me like nothing else ever has. Even though there's this extra training to get through, I'm basically ready. It feels like hummingbird wings are tickling my skin as I try to fall asleep that night.

It's still dark out when I wake the next morning to begin my preparations. This is a ritual I've performed since I was a teenager, and it's soothing to go through the steps: when I step out of the shower, Jane is just setting a steaming cup of espresso down on the bathroom counter. I drink it down before brushing my teeth—can't show up with coffee breath —blow-drying my hair and putting on my makeup. By the time I step into the panties I bought yesterday, their black and pink fabric little more than a whisper against my legs, I'm fully awake and starting to get excited in spite of myself.

Why would a man go to so much trouble to determine my outfit if he wasn't going to see it himself? And how could he hand his untouched bride off to strangers for erotic finishing?

He couldn't. He wouldn't. He's going to be there, I tell myself. I'm going to be with him. And it will all be worth it. Arousal blooms in my belly and spreads throughout my body, warm and sweet like honey. I know I look as perfect as I have molded myself to be on the outside, and I can't wait for this man to crack that candy shell, to touch my molten core. Underneath my dress, my nipples stiffen with anticipation, and I can't believe it: I've never even met this man, but he already has me responding to him more helplessly than anyone I've met before.

I arrive at the address he provided exactly on time. I'm acutely aware of my whole body as I step through the front doors: the scrap of tulle between my legs, and the shape of my breasts under the cling of my dress. Is this what it feels like to be a woman?

Then I lock eyes with the receptionist sitting under a large sign that says Agency M. She looks like Angelina Jolie's younger sister: her dark hair is wavy and impossibly glossy, and her mouth is a lush red pout. She smiles and stands, and I can see that her heels are even higher than mine are. I'm not intimidated by very many people, but this woman has clearly been trained much the same way I have: to be impeccable. She just also manages to be wildly sexy at the same time. I try to ignore the tiny seed of jealousy that plants itself in my heart. Is this the kind of woman my husband is usually surrounded by? Will I be enough for him in comparison?

"Juliette Newmont," she says. It's not a question.

I nod.

"Follow me."

Our heels click across the marble floors as she leads me through the building. The whole place smells like lilies and leather, jasmine and tobacco—a heady mix of masculine and feminine that's echoed in the gleaming, well-polished wood of the furniture, the gilt edging on the tray of cut-crystal glasses that sit next to a wet bar in a small, private lobby. Every detail is exquisite and considered; if I didn't have to keep up, I would want to stop to examine a half-dozen things in our brief walk. Everything that isn't leather and wood is gold or platinum; nothing is glass that could be crystal. As we walk, I realize I'm glad my husband told me how he wanted me to look here, so I don't have to worry about whether or not I fit into this perfectly set scene.

The receptionist leads me to a small conference room. I hold my breath as I walk through the door, and then exhale slowly. No one's in there, waiting for me. Yet.

She closes the door behind me without saying anything

else, leaving me alone in the room's thick quiet. It's just as
beautifully appointed as the rest of the building: lit by white
porcelain sconces shaped like abstract tulips that throw
warm light onto the charcoal walls. The art is original—I
recognize a Picasso at a glance, the Cubist woman with her
mixed-perspective face as discombobulated and confused as
I feel. Heavy drapes block out the sun from the windows at
the far end of the room. A vase of orchids sits at the far end
of a glossy chestnut table, their blooms almost unbearably
delicate and natural amidst all of the opulence they're
surrounded by.

At my end of the table, there's a silver tray with a note-
card on top. When I get close enough, I can see that it reads,
*Remove your underwear. Place them on the tray. Put your elbows
on either side of the tray and wait with this note in your teeth.*

Well. That's...straightforward enough. I slip my underwear down my legs again, stepping carefully so it doesn't
snag on the heels of my shoes as I pull it all the way off and
place it on the tray. Then I put the note in my teeth and do as
I've been told.

If I was aware of myself before, that was nothing on what
it feels like to know I'm basically half naked in a stranger's
office, my hips tilted up in a posture of submission, bare ass
just visible beneath my skirt. Whoever walks in will be able
to see me—be able to touch me if he wants to, slip his fingers
right inside of me while I stand here, exposed.

The thought is surprisingly hot, and I feel it between my
legs—the pressure and pulse that flared at the lingerie
boutique yesterday comes back, and this time it stays, steady
and insistent. A shiver ripples over my skin, leaving goosebumps in its wake. I'm not sure if I want my underwear back
on or if I'm glad it's off already.

But after a while, the feeling fades. With my weight
tipped forward, my feet are out of position in my heels; I can

stand in them for hours, all day if I have to, but this isn't quite standing. My jaw aches from holding the note, and my elbows feel bruised against the wood.

Still, I wait. I know how to endure discomfort, how to fix my face and body so that they give nothing away. I've charmed diplomats with heels scraped bloody from stiff shoes, and eaten dinners in dresses so tight I could barely breathe. *You're good at everything*, Daddy said to me yesterday, and so I will be good at this.

I just wish there was a clock on the wall, so I could know how much time has passed. It feels like a lot. Like, too much. Like maybe he got held up, or forgot about me, or forgot to tell someone to tell me he was running late.

I am extraordinarily well-trained, but I'm not a robot. Eventually, boredom and curiosity do me in, and I let the note fall to the table, where you can see the indentations my teeth made in the cardstock, proof of how long I waited and how hard I tried. I stand up and rub my arms idly while I walk around the room to get my blood flowing again. The table has small drawers set into its side at each seat, and I pop a couple of them open, just to see a bunch of neatly stacked notepads and pens. I'm not a snooper by nature, but sometimes you need to know something, and if no one is going to tell you, this is the only way. Any clues I have now will help me be a better wife, I rationalize; they'll tell me what to expect, and how to mold myself to my husband, if he ever gets here.

I've just snapped another one shut when the door opens and *he* walks in.

The only way to describe him is, massive—not his actual size, which hovers around six foot two—but his presence. The feeling of him. The force of this man in a room is so intense, I sense him before I see him. His broad shoulders fill out every corner of his perfectly tailored suit. His dark hair is carefully slicked back, and a set of green eyes rake over me with an appraising indifference. He's as curtly disinterested in me as if I was just another piece of furniture. I get the distinct sense that I'm being assessed.

I had thought I might impress my new tutor, or, if that failed, at least charm him, but as soon as I see this man, I know both plans are hopeless. He doesn't look like a man who can be teased or tempted. He radiates authority; he's stern and commanding, completely in control of himself and his world.

A hot thrill races through me, licking along the line of my spine. This is it.

This is *him.*

The only other man I've ever met who can hold a room this way is my father. This is exactly the kind of man he would have promised me to. This is no tutor. *This* is my husband.

He looks like a walking dream. He fits perfectly into the life I've pictured for myself: I can imagine sunning myself next to him on private beaches, rubbing sunscreen onto that broad back. Sitting by his side at dinner parties, fixing him a drink after work. Allowing that mouth to open mine, and one of his muscular thighs to part my legs and *press.* I have made myself a perfect wife, and here, at last, is my perfect match: a man who is worth the life I've dedicated to pleasing him.

I half expect a proposal—I know we just met and Daddy said I had more to learn, but he's *here*, so why wait?

Then I realize that his face is not that of a man about to ask a woman a question that will change her life. Instead, his full mouth is set in a flat line, and I start to feel unsettled.

"I'm...I'm Juliette..." I stammer out, hoping to break his silence with my own. Before I've finished the first syllable, I know it was the wrong thing to do. He knows perfectly well who I am. This man doesn't wander into rooms by accident. "You're…"

He doesn't answer me. He doesn't say anything, and the quiet between us seems to stretch even longer than my time at the table did.

Finally, he says, "Your underwear is on the tray."

Did I misunderstand somehow? The note was on the table when I came in. "You asked me to…"

"My Client asked for more than that."

Oh no. The warmth that flooded my body the moment I saw him retreats, and I am cold and small and lost. *My Client.* Does that mean he really is a tutor, and not my husband?

Then the rest of the sentence hits me. *My Client asked for more than that.*

Is this all some sort of test? Have I already failed?

He keeps talking, his tone perfectly level. "There's no point in working with you if you're going to insist on disobedience," he says. "And actually…" He takes a seat at the head of the table, his powerful frame making it look delicate, almost silly. He flips open a folder, and looks at it instead of me. "There's no point in working with you at all, if you aren't what we were led to believe."

I'm so shocked I respond before I can compose myself. "I am! I am! I'm a virgin," I tell him. It's true. No one's ever touched me anywhere—I've barely even touched myself. Though I have a feeling I'm going to need to, once I get home from this. It's not the fact that my underwear is on the table that makes me feel naked in front of this man, as bare as I've ever been with anyone.

"Is that the most important thing you have to offer?"

I only know one answer. "…Yes?"

He looks me over again, and doesn't seem any more impressed by me than he did the first time.

"Yes, *Master,*" he says.

"Do you not have a name?" I ask, and before I'm even done, I know I shouldn't have.

"You'd be a lousy lay no matter what. How do I know that? Because I gave you a position, and you bounced around the room like a cocker spaniel." He pauses to let my shame sink deep. "You haven't earned my name."

I know I shouldn't argue with him, but I can't help myself. "I hardly *bounced*," I say. No one's ever called me a bad student before. Probably because I've never *been* a bad student before. Does he know how long I waited? Does he think I'm just his to command at his leisure, a doll he can leave however he likes? "You were late," I remind him. "You couldn't have meant for me to sit there like that for half an hour!"

"I meant to test you. And you failed. Now—"

I don't want to hear the rest of the sentence. I go flying out the door, leaving my underwear behind, tears blinding me to everything as I race back through that sumptuous lobby, by the beautiful receptionist with her perfectly composed face, and out the front door.

My father is going to be so disappointed in me. I wasn't good enough. I messed it up. I've always been his princess; I've earned his love by being perfect at everything I've tried, and yet now, at this last, most crucial juncture, I ruined it. I wore the right outfit but I did the wrong thing, and in the back seat of the car that takes me home, I sob my broken heart out.

Will Daddy ever forgive me?

Worse still: how will my husband possibly want me now?

2
_____

I SPEND the rest of the day on the Newmont compound, wandering around the guesthouse I call home, trying to shake the sense that I've just doomed myself and my family. My phone doesn't ring, which gives me plenty of time to imagine Daddy's disappointment while I pace, my bare feet nearly soundless on the highly polished floors.

I circle my room, trailing my fingertips along the sweet pink of the walls, the tops of the chairs that feel like some else's, and look out the window onto a garden where Bruce, the brutish head caretaker, barks orders to the two gardeners clipping the hedges. My father's staff grooms with the same precision they use to care for the thoroughbreds in the stables.

The swish of my skirt against my legs is an unbearable reminder of my failure, so I take it off, remembering the underwear I left behind.

What does the Master think of that? Is he turned on? Or disgusted?

I try not to think about it as I change out of my morning outfit and into my favorite loungewear, a pair of oversized silk pajamas Daddy had custom-made for me in Paris the year I turned nineteen. I had hoped they would comfort me, but packing up the dress and heels, the barely worn lingerie—sans panties—I feel sick with fear and regret. Was that it? Is it all over now? In the bathroom, I make sure to put away everything I used this morning; the mascara and lipstick that I daubed on so carefully feel almost accusing. I wasn't paying attention to the right things.

I know that now.

From the bathroom I walk into the sitting room and instantly wish that I hadn't. There, behind the sofa, sits a portrait of my mother, painted when she was about my age. We have the same ash-blonde hair and heart-shaped faces; I've always flattered myself that I looked like her, but today, all I can see is how beautiful she was, and how perfectly self-possessed.

I'm just her shadow, her reflection distorted in a stained, pitted mirror. I'm almost glad she didn't live to witness my failure, but I can't stand even this portrait seeing me humiliated. It feels like her spirit will know, somehow, that her daughter is an embarrassment. I thought I'd cried myself out this morning but tears start coming again, choking me on my own thick sadness.

Of course I failed, I find myself thinking. *Look at you, crying like a little girl in her little girl room. This is pathetic, Juliette.*

So I do what I always do when I'm lonely: go to find Jane. I could ring for her, but I know that if I stay in this house alone I'll just keep crying, so instead I head out to the back of the property, where the carriage house she works from is located.

Jane is technically my hired companion, but since she's also my only companion, she's become my friend, too. We've grown up together, and I'm always grateful for her calmness and practicality—though she has a wicked sense of humor, too, that she deploys in the most unexpected moments.

She answers her door almost as soon as I knock; she's dressed casually, wearing a navy silk Saint Laurent blouse I gave her last year, after I decided the color suited her better than it did me. Jane's hair is thick, curly red, which beautifully complements her freckle-dotted white skin, and the blue is striking even when she's paired it with slacks and bare feet. *At least I did one thing right*, I think, but that's too small a comfort.

"Oh, Juliette," Jane says when she sees my face. As always, she knows exactly what I need: without saying another word, she takes me gently by the elbow and guides me towards the backyard. Her quiet presence soothes me, as does the sunshine and the feeling of the plush grass under my feet. It's warm enough today that we can roll up our pant legs, sit at the lip of the pool, and put our legs in the water. The sensation of it lapping against my calves and my ankles brings me back to myself somewhat, makes me feel less panicked. I close my eyes, wishing I'd thought to bring sunglasses out with me.

"Do you want to talk about it?" she asks.

It all comes bursting out of me in a wave. I tell her about how excited I was when I got dressed this morning; I admit to my high, foolish hopes. I tell her about the beauty of the receptionist and the luxury of the office, and how undone I felt in the presence of my mentor. "I know I haven't met a lot of men," I tell her. "But he was—it was something else. It was like nothing I'd ever felt before. Like my body was liquid. Like he could undress me just by looking at me."

Then I remember what he did instead, which was to dismantle me with criticism thirty seconds after we'd met.

"And you're sure he's not your husband?" Jane's voice is hushed with awe, like I'm telling her a fairy tale, and I wish so much that I was. That this story ended with a ring on my finger and his lips pressed against mine.

"I'm sure," I tell her grimly. "I mean, I almost hope he's not, because then, after that, I screwed everything up." I detail my humiliation: how he caught me disobedient and snooping, and how I ran away at the first sign of trouble.

"So who is he?" Jane asks.

"I'm supposed to call him Master."

Jane's breath catches softly in her throat, and I'm relieved that she seems to find this strange situation a little bit arousing, too. "Even though he isn't your husband?"

I lean back on my hands and look up at the sky, its deep, full blue, wishing it could just swallow me up. "It doesn't matter now," I tell her. "I was stupid. I ruined everything."

"Juliette," she says. "I'm sure you didn't—"

"I did," I snap, and I instantly feel terrible, but she doesn't contradict me again.

BY THE TIME I walk into Daddy's dining room in the evening, I'm so nervous I'm almost shaking. I've changed again, made sure to put on one of my father's favorite outfits, a beaded champagne silk Chanel dress he picked up for me during his last New York trip. I want to look perfect on the outside, even as I'm still shaken to my core on the inside. But he barely glances at me as I enter, instead signaling to Eloise, the cook, that she can start bringing in our plates.

I take my seat at the opposite end of the table from him. Usually sitting in the hostess's seat makes me feel important, like I matter enough to help him anchor this long table and enormous house, but tonight I just feel anxious. I wish I was close enough to him to read his facial expressions more clearly.

Eloise sets down our salads, the delicate greens flecked by hazelnuts and nasturtium blossoms, and I will my body to obey me: fork in hand, I assemble a small bite, but when I try to swallow it, my throat feels like it's been shut tight. I manage to eat less than half of it before she comes back to clear.

"Not hungry?" my father asks.

Of course he noticed. He notices everything.

"No." It's like this morning washed away every ounce of my training. My voice sounds exactly as young and terrified as I feel.

"You should eat," he says, "because I expect you'll want your energy to go back there and *clean up your mess!*" He roars the last four words so loudly that my water glass shakes with vibrations; he rises from his seat. The chair scraping on the marble floor punctuates his rage, echoing, almost, the friction lingering in the air between us.

I can't stand it. Any attempt at composure abandons me, and I burst into tears as he strides out of the room.

Does he want me to go back now? Tomorrow? It doesn't matter. I can't. I cannot. The idea of showing up just to be told to leave, that I've ruined things beyond repair, is intolerable. I'd rather pretend there's some way of fixing it than to admit to the truth, which is that if my husband doesn't want me now, well…maybe he's right about that.

So I run to our little house and hide there, wondering if Jane will bring me a plate from the kitchen. She does that sometimes, when she knows I haven't eaten enough at dinner. But no one comes, and eventually I put on a night-gown and fall asleep, tear tracks still salty on my cheeks, and my belly tight with hunger and fear.

———

WHEN I WAKE AGAIN, it's dark except for the moonlight coming through my window, which illuminates the man standing over me.

Not just any man.

It's him.

The Master.

He's here.

I'm too fuzzy-headed to process any of this. "Get out!" I yelp, clutching my bedsheets around me as tightly as possible. The nightgown I fell asleep in is made of fine, thin cotton, and I wonder if he saw the shape of my nipples or the shadows of my breasts before I woke.

"I'm not here to obey *you*," he says, and proves it by taking a seat at the edge of my bed. "If you want a second chance at earning your husband, who has set this up so carefully for you, even though you behaved like a brat…"

He pauses, and I nod enthusiastically, not trusting my voice. I didn't think this was fixable, but if it is, I'll do anything.

"Good," he says. "Then get yourself over my knee right now."

"I'm sorry?"

"Don't make me ask you twice, ever again."

I won't, I swear to myself I'll never make him do that but I'm terrified that I'll make a wrong move.

I can't just sit here, so I unclench my fingers one by one and let the blanket drop. Then I crawl across his lap, situating myself so that I'm lying facedown, my ass in the air and his firm, strong thighs beneath me.

My hips tilt up without my permission, and I'm glad I can bury my face in my quilt so that he can't see that I'm on fire with shame and need. What must it look like to him, the shapes and shadows of my body, half revealed by the gauzy fabric of my nightgown? My hips tilting up like an invitation to a man I barely know. Does it feel as delicious to him as it does to me? Or does he just see a weak and lazy little girl, a job to be completed and nothing else?

He spanks me once, so hard it startles the breath out of me. Then he does it again.

"You don't speak to me that way," he instructs, punctuating the sentence with another smack. "I'll be your mentor." *Smack.* "I'll oversee your education." *Smack.* "I said *oversee.*" *Smack.* By this point my blood is roaring in my ears, and I'm praying he can't feel me getting wet through the thin fabric of my nightgown. My ass must be pink, maybe red, raw from his touch, but he doesn't let up. "Your teachers," *smack,* "hand-selected for their specialties," *smack* "will" *smack* "guide" *smack* "you." After a last *smack*, he pauses.

Into his silence, I gasp out, "Yes, sir."

He spanks me again, over and over, relentless, and I feel the world opening up around me as he holds me in place. He's merciless. I want the night to swallow me, or maybe I want him to. Finally my brain clears enough to tell me why he hasn't let up yet.

"Yes," I moan. "Master."

He stops touching me instantly. "You can get up."

I pull myself to standing, my ass smarting and my pussy aching, as confused and ashamed and aroused as I've ever been. I didn't know my body could feel this much. Every inch of my skin is sensitive, even though he barely touched me anywhere. I'm overcome by a wild desire to climb into his lap again, to lick my way into his mouth and sink onto his cock, let him fill me up to the hilt, bruise my pussy the way he's just bruised up my ass. I barely recognize myself with this wanton need that's risen in me.

I have to know who's done this to me.

"You're really not going to tell me your name?" I ask.

He stands up, swift and efficient, and throws a business

card on the bed. "Your first lesson is in obedience," he says. "I'll see you tomorrow morning at nine-oh-seven, sharp. I trust you will be neither early nor late."

I wait until he's gone to turn on my bedside lamp and see what the card says.

It's for The Bogatsvo Dance Studio, and for a moment, all thoughts of how my body feels are forgotten. Vlad Bogatsvo is *legendary*. My ballet teachers growing up were all French, and they never went easy on me, but even they whispered when they discussed the intensity and militarism of Russian methods.

Why is this what Master has chosen? Does he know that I dance? Does my husband?

I turn off the light and lie down again, but the moon seems bright through the window now, and my mind is too busy to sleep. No man has ever touched me that intimately before, and I don't know what to make of it, or my reaction to it.

The spanking hurt, of course, but it also felt…good. Even now, with the force of him gone from the room, I remember how badly I wanted more: wanted him to pull up my night-gown to smack my bare skin, to slip his fingers inside of me and feel just how wet I was for him. And then—God, I wanted all of him. Is this what my husband wants for me? To lust after another man? To let this stranger do whatever he wants with my body?

We're barely a day into training, and I'm already impossibly mixed up and confused. What's going to happen tomorrow? Will I pass the next test, even though I failed the first one so badly?

3

IN THE MORNING, I rescue my pointe shoes from the back of my closet. It's been a while, but luckily this pair is already broken in the way I like them, ribbons sewn and soles scraped and softened. There's a soothing familiarity to tying myself into them and sitting down to give myself a quick pre-warmup stretch.

Except that as soon as I hit the floor, my bottom screams in protest, and so do I. "Ouch!"

Jane, who's been gathering the rest of my things for my dance bag, whirls around at my cry. "Are you okay?"

"I'm fine." I stand up again, but the ache doesn't disappear, and all the memories of last night come rushing back to me. What it felt like to be overpowered in my own bed, at a man's mercy. How much I liked it in the moment.

Well, I hate it now.

"You sure?" Jane asks.

"I mean, I'm not *fine*," I say, rolling over one toe and then another to warm up my feet and ankles. "After a lifetime of following every single rule, doing everything that was asked of me, trying to be as perfect as possible, I'm being given a series of *impossible* tests by a man who won't even tell me his name."

Jane nods. "I'm sorry," she says, and rubs my shoulder briefly before going back to her duties. I watch her as she puts my water bottle in the monogramed Hermes bag, along with a makeup bag containing extra hair ties and bobby pins. I'm grateful for her companionship, but as always, a little sad, too. Jane and I have spent our lives together, but she's my friend, and I am her job. I wish there were someone else here to listen to me—someone who wanted to, instead of being compelled to.

But here we are. I sink into a demi plié once, wincing at the pull on my glutes, and then again, concentrating on keeping my stomach pulled in and my face expressionless. Better.

Now a grand plié.

"What do I need to learn about obedience?" I hear myself asking. "I've been obedient my entire life. What will I ever get out of this? Is there a reward, or do I just roll over forever?" I try a little combination, ending in a jeté, just to show off. "How lovely for my husband to have a custom-built wife."

Jane zips the bag closed and turns to face me. "Can I ask you something?" she says.

"Of course."

"I...overheard something last night," she says. "You were talking to a man in your room."

"Master."

If Jane is surprised that Master was in my room at three in the morning, she doesn't let on. Discretion is one of the first lessons a companion learns, and it's one of her strongest skills. Her voice is just a bit trembly when she says, "Then, after...it sounded like he was spanking you."

I go crimson. God, were we that loud? Who else could

have heard us? Jane's guesthouse isn't far away from mine, but it's not close enough to easily hear skin striking skin. Maybe it was the wind in the yard, and no one else in the house was disturbed by it. I did fall asleep with my window open.

"I just wanted to know…what did it feel like?" she asks.

I'm as pink as my leotard; at this rate, I'll still be blushing when I get to the studio. How can I possibly admit the truth? "It hurt," I say. "He's strong."

Jane nods. Her eyes are trained on the floor. I hope she doesn't think she did wrong by asking me.

"But also," I say, because I have to confess, and there's no one else to hear me, "it kind of felt…good. I had this weird fluttery feeling. Like…nerve endings I didn't know I had."

Jane nods, a sly smile spreading slowly across her face. "So it was hot."

"I don't know if I can say that." Now I'm terrified that everything is a test I'm failing, a rubric I'm failing to even see clearly. "Is it cheating on my future husband to enjoy a spanking from my mentor?"

Jane always trusts me when I don't trust myself. She laughs, and shakes her head. "Surely not. Now come on. Are you ready to go show them what you can really do?"

I am. I exchange my pointe shoes for flats, pull on leg warmers and a sweater to keep my muscles warm, and when I'm ready, I sling my dance bag over my shoulder, reaching up to make sure my bun is perfectly smooth one last time before we head out.

"I'm going to show them this is a waste of everyone's time," I say. I have to get my confidence back. I can't just collapse in the studio. I've worked too hard and too long to imagine myself to be less than I am now. "I know how to dance en pointe, and I *am* obedient. I just didn't understand Master was testing me. Now that I know, I'll get it right."

"Exactly," Jane says.

I smile at her as we walk out to the waiting Bentley together. "We'll get this over with and be on our way to a girls' weekend in the Maldives in no time."

4

THAT CONFIDENCE LASTS for about five minutes after I meet my instructor, Vlad.

I know what to expect, of course—Russian ballet instruction demands a kind of regimented, exacting obedience that not everyone can achieve. I wasn't even allowed to start my training in ballet until I was seven, because before then, I would have been too young to understand how to isolate my muscles, to work towards the perfection that would be demanded of me.

But once I began, I threw myself at it like I do with everything, practicing over and over again until my fouettés were crisp enough to pass muster under my teachers' exacting eyes. Until recently, I've always thrived under pressure, and I'm almost excited to show Master what I can do.

When I walk into the studio, it's beautiful—a gorgeous black Steinway piano sits in one corner, with a silent, sour-faced woman poised on its bench, ready to play. No Angelina lookalikes here, and I'm silently relieved not to have to compete.

A wall of east-facing windows lets in the morning's light. The other three walls are covered in floor-to-ceiling mirrors, and they reflect dozens of Juliettes around me, as slender and nervous as rabbits, stepping through the studio doors.

A man is standing in the center of the floor, waiting for me, his legs in a perfect fifth position. He's wearing all black, a stark contrast to my tights and leotard, which are the soft pink of a seashell's curve. I always like to wear light colors when I dance—I think it pairs nicely with my blonde hair, and makes me look just a little lighter when I jump.

The man is undeniably young and handsome, and the cling of his outfit highlights every long, lean muscle in his dancer's body. I was never interested in the boys I danced with when I was younger—and, by and large, they weren't interested in me. But I can't deny that the sight of this man makes me buzz, a faint echo of the way Master made me feel, my body helplessly attuned to his.

This time, at least, I know to wait for instructions.

"I'm Vlad," he says. "You will call me *Instruktor*." He lays the accent heavily on the third syllable as you do in Russian. "You warmed up already, yes?" He barely waits for my nod before saying, "Good. You will begin at the barre."

I take my place along the wall, glad to have the wooden beam to rest my hand on so it doesn't tremble. He nods to the woman at the piano and she begins to play as he commands my movements.

"First position," he says.

This is the most basic thing in the world, a position I could manage even as a first grader: I stand with my heels together, feet turned out, one hand on the barre and the other held, cupped palm up, in front of me. I feel my posture fall into alignment; my hips are surprisingly supple for a few months out of practice.

Usually what comes next is a demi plié. Instead, I get a torrent of criticism.

"Your tailbone is misaligned," he says. "Because your stomach is out of position. Correct it."

I take a quick, covert glance in the mirror, but my body looks the same as it always does. My turnout is flawless, my tailbone is down, and my stomach is as flat as it's going to get. Still, I try to drop my butt another little bit, glad I practiced not wincing when I use those muscles.

Vlad motions for the pianist to stop playing.

"Olga, you may leave," he says, and she quietly slips out of the room, leaving us alone.

"That is," he says, "a pathetic attempt."

My ass hurts, but my pride hurts more. "I might be a little rusty," I say, hoping to buy myself just a sliver of lenience. "But I was just traveling, and I haven't had a chance to really practice in a few months. I'm sure by the end of the session I'll be—"

"What is wrong with you cannot be fixed in an hour."

"It's just first position!"

"I'm not sure I want to see second."

I'm determined to prove him wrong, so I step my feet wide and drop into a grand plié, willing him to notice that I can get my hips even with my knees without tucking or sticking my butt out. Madame Charcot always said that my arms were my best feature, long and graceful; I had an instinct, she told me, for how to hold my hands. Now I raise them over my head and rise from the plié all the way into a relevé, balancing on the boxes of my toe shoes, perfectly en pointe.

"Unimpressive. Back to the bar," Vlad snaps. "We will begin with your fundamentals. Do you know where your coccyx is?"

Before I can respond, his hand is at the base of my spine, pushing my tailbone towards the floor. The strong, self-assured pressure so near my bruised skin is confusing, and I feel myself press helplessly into his palm.

Just as quickly as he touched me, though, he pulls away again, circling around to size up my front. *Focus*, I remind myself. *Show them what you can do.*

"Do you know where the abdominal muscles are?" Vlad asks, one fingertip drawing a line from my belly button to just between my breasts. My nipples are hard, and the built-in bra of my leotard does nothing to hide them. "Ah," he says, seeing them. "So at least one part of you knows how to pay attention."

"I—" I start to stammer out an excuse—something about the air conditioning, maybe—but he's already moved on. *It's nothing he hasn't seen before*, I remind myself. He probably isn't even interested in my nipples. Thank God he didn't understand that they're a response to him.

Which is so inappropriate. *He is not my husband*, I remind myself.

God, what is happening to me? Ever since I met Master, I've been ready to be turned on at the slightest touch.

Vlad taps at the top of my sternum, and, seeing me respond, he presses his palm there, warm skin bare against mine where the u neck of my leotard reveals my décolletage. The physical pressure works, and I feel myself straightening and firming, even as my traitorous mind is begging him to put that hand on my breasts and then between my legs; to cup me there, to feel how wet and warm I am for him. It's humiliating to be moved around like a child, but it reminds me of Master's slaps last night—there's something undeniably, shamefully hot about it, too.

I feel like the session is going marginally better as I sink into another plié, Vlad's hand still on my chest, a distraction I know I can't afford. He must be able to feel me trying to keep myself in check, because he sighs. "Stop resisting," he says. "As long as you resist, you will never dance."

I want to dance. I want to prove myself. I want—my eyes stray guiltily to the bulge in his leggings, which is exactly as defined as his quads and his calves. Master's body is torrentially powerful, but Vlad's compactness has its own appeal. I know he could lift me in the air if he wanted to; he could carry me around this room and make me feel like a feather in his arms.

"Now," he says. "Show me an arabesque."

I kick out a leg behind me, rising slowly to pointe again on my standing foot. I can see the line of my body in the mirror, and it looks graceful enough to me, but again, Vlad is disappointed.

"You don't know where the movement starts," he says. "You have to know where your head is." His hands touch me there before trailing down to pass over every body part he names. "That shows you where the spine goes, how to arch your back. How to use your hips to lengthen that back leg."

He pauses and then strokes the inner thigh of my standing leg, his touch so light I almost can't be sure what's happening. "Use these muscles," he says. "Make them work." His fingers go higher, higher, until I swear they're grazing my seam, taunting me where I want him the most.

Is this really happening? Is this allowed? Master said I had to learn obedience. I'm trapped between anger and need. Before I can make any decisions, Vlad steps back and taps my lifted ankle once. "Down."

I go.

"First position," he says, and when I've done it, he stands behind me and presses his whole body against mine. "You have to feel it everywhere," he says. "Here," my breasts, "here," my hips, "here," definitely my pussy this time. My body flashes hot and cold. I suck in a breath, and I know he hears it.

"In my classroom," Vlad says, "nothing is off-limits. Do you understand that?"

"Yes," I say.

"You will give me everything I ask for," he continues.

"Yes," I repeat. I almost want him to just take me—forget the illusion of a dance lesson and press his cock into me, slow and steady. Fuck me in the mirror and make me watch as he takes me apart.

Who is this girl? I don't recognize myself. But I don't hate it, either.

Instead, Vlad smacks my ass once, the slap landing right on the tender curve of my cheek where the skin is so raw I can't help sucking in another hurt little breath at the sting of it.

"Again," he says, and, of course, I obey.

At home, I've barely shut the door to my room before I'm pulling my tights and leotard down to shove a hand between my legs. The whole session was like that—Vlad criticizing me and then touching me, making me wild with desire as I struggled, uselessly, to please him even once with my dancing. The shame only made everything hotter, and I'm desperate with need by the time my fingers slip between my folds.

I've never felt like this before—like a fire raging out of control, consuming everything in sight. I bend over my bed as I touch myself, bracing myself with my free hand and imagining Vlad doing this for me, both of us too impatient to undress me all the way. His hands would be big enough to cover my breasts, and he would breathe against my neck as he massaged my clit, his cock hard and ready between my legs. "You're a terrible dancer," the Vlad in my mind murmurs, "but a perfect slut."

I've never felt this needy before. I've explored my own body, of course, in order to understand it, but that was always...perfunctory. Part of my training. Now I feel like an animal in a rut, dripping all over myself as I fuck myself on my fingers, wishing they were bigger—wishing they were him.

"That's right," I imagine Vlad murmuring. "Legs apart for me. Good girl. Don't be afraid to spread."

I don't mean to, but then I think of Master: how I bent over his desk like this yesterday, my ass an offering I was supposed to make for him. What would have happened if I'd stayed?

I force my mind back to Vlad, but I'm spinning out of control, my orgasm pulling me under, and the voice in my head sounds much more like Master's as he urges me on. "Come for me," he rumbles, "now," and this time, alone in my room, I do exactly as I'm told.

Afterwards, my body is finally loose and relaxed. I take a long shower and by the time I get out, Jane is at my door, asking if I want a snack. I'm starving, so I tell her to ask Eloise to make me a plate of crudité while I get dressed.

The last thing Vlad said to me today was "Tomorrow, again," sounding bored and almost annoyed about it, so I lay out another leotard and pair of tights for myself, making a mental note that I'll want to buy more if this goes on for much longer.

I know I shouldn't be, but I'm almost looking forward to tomorrow's lesson. Maybe Vlad will say nice things about me to Master—I might not have impressed him, but I stayed the whole time, and I did try. And he wasn't shy about putting his hands on me, so maybe he enjoyed that part?

That would be good, I think. I deserve a little reward for going along with this ridiculous thing.

5

THE BUMP of the town car passing over cobblestoned streets no longer makes me wince—it's been weeks since Master came to me in the night, weeks since I've seen or heard from him directly. Instead, it's been sessions with Vlad every day, endless hours of ankle exercises and complaints about my extension, practicing the most basic postures over and over and fucking *over*, attending to details so minute I sometimes have trouble following what he wants me to do. It took two weeks before we were allowed to leave the barre, and I had hoped that when he started choreographing a routine for me it meant that he was pleased with my progress, but so far, nothing I've done seems to have impressed him at all. He criticizes my pirouettes as vigorously as he did my pliés.

Meanwhile, every muscle in my body has been sore for so long I've forgotten what it felt like to live any other way, and that pedicure I was so proud of has surrendered to blisters and bleeding. I've given up on fixing it. My hair is semi-permanently in a bun, and I can't help wondering why my husband dressed me so exquisitely for my first meeting with Master, so he could let me look like this.

The worst part of all of it, though, is the touching. Vlad seems to know exactly how much I like it when he puts his hands on me, and now he only does it when I'm performing exactly as he wants me to. Every day, we begin with warmups—first position, second, third fourth fifth, pliés and grand pliés, facing front and then back. They're the same exercises I've been performing since I was a child, and he won't let me skip a second of them. It's boring and annoying, except when he's pleased with me, and then it's torture as he smooths a palm over my ribs or cups the curve of my ass, murmuring, "Yes. Like that." I've given up on trying to pretend it doesn't affect me; we both know I'm wet for him, and we both know he just wants to torment me for as long as he can.

So every time I deviate even the tiniest bit—forget myself, and perform an English fouetté instead of a Russian one, or miss the count in a series of pirouettes by even one—he's distant and glowering, making me feel like I'm barely worthy of his attention, let alone his hands. After a few days he brought in a cane that he uses to touch me when I'm particularly disappointing him, like he can't even bear to let his skin come into contact with mine. The smacks from the wood are humiliating—but they're also a little thrilling, because they remind me so much of Master's spanks. I leave every session sweating and wet and frustrated; I barely even enjoy touching myself anymore, because it feels like such a pale imitation of what I actually want. But I also can't stop, because otherwise I'll explode.

When I was younger, I had hazy visions of cuddling on beaches with someone as handsome as my Latin tutor; by the time I was a teenager, I pictured my husband being so overwhelmed at the first sight of me on our wedding day that he would take me up against a wall in a library or a hallway, stripping me of my virginity with tender desperation. But I never could have guessed at this: at Master and Vlad, and their spankings and criticisms. And how much I crave them. How they make me crazier than any easy tenderness ever could.

I did well yesterday, making it through the end of the routine he choreographed for me even though he critiqued my jeté in the middle; when we went over it after, he rewarded me with so much contact that I'm still a little dizzy from it this morning. It's only the jolting of the car that keeps me from drifting away into a dream, and even still, I forget to keep checking the dashboard clock until it's almost too late. The next time I glance over, it's 8:21 a.m.

Shit.

I grab my phone and dial, praying that the number will flip at the exact right second. I've almost got this down to a science by now, but it depends on whether the receptionist picks up after three rings, or two.

It's two today, thank God, and it's 8:22 exactly when she says, "Hello, Juliette. Master isn't in right now. Call him again tomorrow at 2:09 p.m."

Then she hangs up.

I barely have time to breathe a sigh of relief before I get annoyed again. I've been trying to call Master for weeks, too. The first set of instructions came on my second day of dance lessons; they said to call at 1:45 p.m., and when the receptionist told me he was out, I assumed he was busy. She told me to try again at 12:01 p.m. the following day. I was early—my call came through at noon, because I was stupid and eager, and thought he might be impressed by that. The receptionist told me he wasn't available, and that was that, with no exact time to call the next day, and that was how I learned that early is as bad as late.

Since then, it's followed the same pattern: a call timed perfectly gets me instructions to call again tomorrow, which is better than the silence that awaits when I'm off by even a few seconds.

Between the two of them, Master and Vlad, I feel like I'm losing my mind. However annoyed I thought I was when this all started is nothing compared to where I'm at now. I get wanting to train me in obedience, especially after I messed up that first test, but haven't I proven myself enough by now? I'm not going to join the Bolshoi. I don't *actually* have to be a flawless ballerina. I just don't understand what they are trying to get me to do.

The car pulls up to the studio, and the breath of air I get on the way inside makes up my mind. I could be lounging by the pool right now, spending these last summer days working on my tan, or learning a new skill instead of needlessly perfecting an old one. Instead, I'm trapped in a hall of mirrors with an instructor who refuses to concede an inch, being teased and disciplined but never told how to get better. And I'm going to give him a piece of my mind.

Except that when I step into the studio, Vlad isn't alone.

Instead, there are a dozen men seated along the far wall, each of them wearing a dark suit and a careless aura of power. They're all handsome enough, and I'd take any one of them for a husband, I think—especially if it meant I could get the hell out of this torture chamber.

Then I see him.

Master.

And everyone else in the room disappears.

Vlad doesn't say anything to them, or about them, just nods me in the direction of the barre and says, "Begin."

He's usually allowed me to get through the first few minutes of warmup without criticism lately, but today he's sighing before I've even gotten my feet into third position. "Your hips," he says, jerking me into place and then smacking me on the ass. "And that core is an abomination. It's like you haven't heard a word I said these past few weeks. Stop thinking about your cunt and start *dancing*, Juliette."

I know I'm blushing, and I sneak a glance at the men, but they're all impassive, as if they expected this. So clearly, this is what my husband wants, even if I don't understand why. One of them has a head of blonde curls; he's the youngest, I think, and probably the most muscular under his suit. Maybe it's just his youth, but he looks slightly more friendly than the rest of them, and I try to catch his eye as I sink into a grand plié.

Vlad pokes me in the back of my neck with the cane. "Focus."

After that, Blondie won't return my gaze. As I go through the rest of the exercises, I try each of them in turn—the one with a distinct scowl, and the one wearing a heavy gold ring on his thumb, the one with hints of ginger in his well-trimmed beard and even, at last, Master's stormy eyes. I get nothing. No engagement, no response.

Vlad tosses the cane aside in frustration. "Stop slouching," he says, palming my breasts as he presses my ribs back where he wants them. When he steps away, my nipples are visibly hard in my thin leotard, and I'm flushed from effort and his touch and the fact that everyone in the room knows that I can't concentrate because my pussy quivers with want and I'm imagining Vlad forcing me to my knees and taking it.

Vlad can see that I'm rattled, but he doesn't let up; as we continue through the routine, even the tiniest miscue gets a correction, his hands mapping all the ways my body disappoints him, and then putting me exactly where I'm supposed to be instead. When I rise up onto my toes in an arabesque, he smacks my cunt with an open palm and just says, "Come on, Juliette. Spread." I try to do as he commands, and he rewards me with a long stroke there, the pressure so good I have to close my eyes in order not to press back into it. Every one of my muscles hurts, and this sensation is so hot that I can't remember to care.

Is my husband watching right now? What the hell is he thinking of this, and of me?

Then Vlad takes his hand away. "First position," he commands, and I try to reassemble myself. I'm failing and I'm desperately turned on and I'm on display, each of these men witnessing my shame like they're in a business meeting, silent and sedate.

I wonder if Master will spank me after. I wonder if he'll make them watch.

"I think these men are getting thirsty," Vlad says. "You should get them water."

I'm thrilled to get a break, just a moment to collect myself, but then he says, "En pointe, please."

I'm too exhausted to be polite. A laugh escapes my mouth, and I shake my head. I'm happy to be obedient and I'm happy to be whatever my husband wants me to be but I'm not in training to be a *servant*. There have to be some limits. At least one rule. "You know I'm not a waitress, right?" I say.

Wrong move. In unison, every man gets up and files out of the room without giving me a second glance. Master is the first one to go.

6

By the time I get home, all of my shame and anxiety has melted—I'm too tired to feel anything but my bruises and blisters, and the ache that starts in my feet touches every muscle in my body. By the time I've stripped off my leotard and tights, my shamefully damp-crotched panties, Jane has a steaming bath ready for me, the water obscured by a mass of sweet rose-scented bubbles.

I slip into the water and let out a long sigh. I may have ruined everything. I may have failed another test. But I've been wound too tight for too long, and right this second, my body needs to unwind so badly I can't quite bring myself to panic. Instead, I sink and sink into the water, imagining that, one way or another, I'll wake up tomorrow and never have to dance again.

Jane takes my hair out of its bun and brushes it smooth. She doesn't ask for any details about what happened today; she knows how hard the last few weeks have been on me. It's nice to just be quiet with someone for a while, to have her company without feeling like I have to work to earn it.

I'm just starting to wonder if I could fall asleep in the tub when the bathroom door opens, and I'm so startled I sit up.

It's Master.

He's here.

"Jane," he says. "Please excuse us."

His authority is so palpable that she goes almost without question, only shooting me a quick glance as she slips out the door and leaves us alone. I've slunk back into the water again, but most of the bubbles have dissolved at this point, and there's not enough to cover my nakedness. I cross an arm in front of my breasts, but it's not enough, and he won't look away.

"Are you allowed to look at me like this?" I ask, my legs curling in to keep him from seeing everything. "I'm not for your eyes."

Master's voice is as indifferent as ever. "The Client trusts me to turn you into a proper toy however I see fit," he says. "If someone else has played with you first, that's of no matter." I'm expecting a lecture, or another spanking, but instead, he sits on the edge of the tub. His quadriceps flex in his suit fabric and I want him so badly I'm dizzy with it.

"You failed today," he says. "You were too preoccupied with your instructor and your audience to relax."

Does he think I didn't spend the whole car ride home obsessing about this? "I know," I tell him, hoping that will win me a point or two, at least. "I know what I did. I've learned."

"Prove it."

"How?"

"I'm giving you a pop quiz." I can barely nod my agreement before he says, "First, stop covering yourself up like a little girl. You're a woman. Act like it."

I straighten my legs and drop my arm. My nipples are stiff and expectant, and I'm wet already, just from the firmness of his voice. I haven't touched myself yet today, but I can already feel how badly I need to.

"Now part your legs—you can bend your knees if you need to. Don't touch yourself there yet. Instead, I want you to put a hand on your breast. Use your thumb to play with your nipple." He sounds as objective and factual as Vlad taking me through my warmups, demanding first position and then second, plié, demi plié, again, again.

"Now slide that hand down your stomach, between your legs. Just press."

A helpless whimper escapes my lips at the first moment of contact. I've been so turned on all day. Is he going to get me off? Isn't he going to help?

"Just feel yourself," Master says. "You know where your clit is. Where your folds are. You know where you want to touch, right?"

"Yes, Master."

"Good. Get out of the bath."

I stand up carefully, water running off my body as patches of bubbles slide down my arms and legs, their touch featherlight, a whisper, a torture. Whatever he might have missed before he can definitely see now, and I want to cover myself so badly, but Master isn't concerned with that. He's the first man who's ever seen me naked, and he doesn't look remotely interested as he assesses me briefly before nodding, mostly to himself. "Come straddle my thigh," he says. "Facing away from me. Good girl."

I feel terrible about messing up his perfect suit, but he told me what to do, and so I obey, shocked at the feeling of my bare pussy pressed against that starched, stiff fabric, and the hard line of muscle underneath. I see him in the mirror with his hands at his sides, uninterested in touching me.

"Now," he says. "You have five minutes to get yourself off on my leg. No hands, Juliette. I know you know how to use those." I wonder if somehow he knows how often I've touched myself in the last few weeks, how often I've succumbed to orgasm imagining his cock deep inside of me and his hands pinning me down while he forces me to take every inch of him.

But then he says "go," and I stop thinking. Immediately, I give myself over to sensation, rocking my hips and moaning as I feel the relief of friction where I need it most. I've already soaked his suit with my skin, so there's no reason to feel humiliated at how wet I am for him, how I can't help humping him like I'm in heat.

I can feel my orgasm building as I ride him, and I finally look up from the floor to see our reflection in the mirror on the opposite wall. My heart contracts at the sight.

We are surrounded by the gold frame. My body, pale and vulnerable, naked and wet and needy, and him buttoned-up behind me, letting me hump his leg. It's the closest to sex I've ever had, and it's brain-meltingly hot to see the tight pink buds of my nipples and my cheeks the same color, my slender ballerina's body contrasted with the crisp black of his suit, his dark hair and jade green eyes. His size and his power. My white-hot need and his glacial indifference.

"One minute," he says.

Master's been warning me every time another minute passes, and I've been holding back as best I can; when he tells me there's only sixty seconds left, I start to ride him in earnest, but I held back a little too long.

"Fifteen seconds," he says, and when he gets to ten he starts counting down. I'm near tears as I thrust against him, my whole body straining for release, for his praise. My wrung-out leg muscles are shaking and I can barely hold myself up, but I have to. I have to.

Then he says "one," and there's a horrible moment of

silence before I feel the orgasm galloping to me hard as I writhe and pant.

But I'm just seconds too late.

"Stand up," he says, and the orgasm skids to a stop. I can barely manage to straighten my legs under me, but I do. "Turn around." My pussy is pounding and I'm so wrung out I barely have the energy to face him.

"I'm sorry," I whisper.

"You're getting better," he allows. "But you still failed, and I will need to punish you."

Another spanking? Even though I just came, my clit twitches feebly at the thought of his hands on me again.

"You aren't allowed to come until I tell you to," Master says. "For yourself, or anyone else. Don't try touching yourself in bed at night. I'll know."

I don't ask how. He won't tell me. All he wants is my obedience.

"I won't. I swear."

Master nods once, and I'm relieved that he believes me. "Good."

Then he leaves me standing alone in the damp bathroom, pussy raw and empty, body still aching and needy, and all I know is, I'm more confused than ever by what I have and what I want.

7

BY THE TIME JANE RETURNS, I'm sitting in my room in my bathrobe. My hair is in a neat braid and even though I know I'm squeaky clean, I feel… I don't know what I feel.

"I brought you tea," Jane says. She sets the cup and saucer down. The china is mismatched to the house, but one of my favorites from childhood, painted with sweet English roses, but the gold that runs around the rim reminds me of the mirror's edging, and how it framed my body as I gave in to my pleasure and let Master see me come undone. How close I came to pleasing him, and how far I still am from succeeding at one of his tasks.

"Do you want me to leave?" Jane asks.

"No."

"Do you want to…talk about it?"

Jane seemed intrigued when I told her about the spanking, so maybe she won't be too shocked by what just happened. I nod, and she takes her customary seat in the armchair across the room.

"That was Master," I say, perhaps unnecessarily. Who else could he have been?

"He's gorgeous," Jane says. "I can see why—I can see why you feel the way you do about him."

I can't help but giggle. It feels good to be able to talk openly with her, to gossip like the girls we've always been. "Isn't he? God. That body."

"Those eyes," Jane agrees. "I'd do whatever he asked of me, too."

"He was at the studio when I went to dance today," I tell her. "So was my husband."

"Oh my God! Wait a minute! Did you—"

"There were twelve men there to watch me," I explain. "So I don't know which one he was."

"Oh."

"They were all handsome. Any one of them would have been a good match, probably." I remember Blondie's curls, and Ginger Beard's hands, which looked big enough to wrap around my waist easily. There were plenty of men there who seemed like excellent options, but none held a candle to Master's intensity.

"You couldn't tell...anything?" Jane asks.

I shake my head. "I could barely look at them. I was busy dancing. Or trying to, anyway. Vlad was awful today— according to him, I couldn't do a single thing right." I can't quite bring myself to talk about how he manhandled me in front of all of them, letting them see that I could be used like a plaything. More than that, I don't have the strength to tell her that I liked it. "I just hope I didn't disappoint him."

"You did what you were told, right?"

I nod.

"That's the point, then. He doesn't need you to be a perfect ballerina."

"I hope not."

I sip my tea, and its sweet aroma calms me slightly—it's the same French lavender Jane used to make me when I was learning dressage and I would come home shaky after long rides, occasionally bruised after a nasty fall.

"So then what did he come for tonight?"

"He—" How can I describe it? Everything that's happening to me is so new that I barely have words for it, and I'm not sure I want to. I sort of like how it feels to fall into sensation, and let myself fall apart without thinking too much about anything, or how it would feel if anyone else saw me do it.

Still, Jane deserves some kind of answer. "He wanted to give me a chance to try again, to follow his instructions. He made me get out of the bath, naked, and sit on his leg. Straddle it, actually."

Jane gives a little gasp, and even from across the room I can see color rising in her cheeks.

"It was so—Jane, I've never seen anything like it. I felt like a *woman*, sitting there with him. Like he was just so big and strong and serious, and there I was, just —pink all over, you know? Delicate. Breakable. But he wouldn't let me break. He just let me use him for my pleasure." A shudder quakes through me, the aftershock of all of that sensation. "It felt so good. I want to feel that way again."

"So what are you going to do next?"

"Whatever he tells me to do, I guess."

My phone rings, and I go to pick it up. It's my father, of course, and I flinch when I see his name on the caller ID. Has Master already apprised him of what happened today?

"Juliette," he says when I answer. "I hear you're struggling in your lessons."

Fuck. What did Master say? Is there any way to get myself out of this mess? "I'm trying so hard, Daddy. I swear. I'm doing everything I can."

"Well then. You will have to try harder. Because you do

not fail, Juliette. You haven't failed as long as I've known you, and you will not fail now."

He's right. I know he's right. I got back on all of those horses, rode them until I could ride Western and English, sidesaddle and bareback; I've never backed down from a challenge before, and I will not start now. Not when the stakes are this high. Not when I have everything to gain.

"I will not fail," I repeat, trying to believe this as strongly as my father does.

But I do have a question that's been nagging at me for too long, now, that I need to ask. "Daddy," I say. "I promise I will not fail you, or my husband. But I do wonder, why did you teach me so many things and always tell me to speak for myself when he just wants this obedient plaything? Maybe if I understood…"

He cuts me off. "If you have to ask, it means you haven't learned your lesson. You will make me proud. You always have."

He clicks off the line, and I sit there, looking at the phone.

I don't understand why this is happening, but maybe I don't need to. I didn't always understand the point of my lessons when I was younger—surely a man didn't need a wife who knew every type of sailing knot ever invented when most of the people I knew only took to the water in mega-yachts, but that didn't stop me from excelling in them anyway. Sometimes, the point was just to prove myself. Maybe that's all I need to do now.

My father's praise has reignited something within me, and it reminds me of how I did it all those other times. I clung to what I was good at, and built on it; I remembered every nice thing my teachers said, and pretended the negative comments had never happened.

It will be harder with Vlad, but I've already endured weeks of his taunting; I'm sure I've heard his worst, and even if I haven't, it doesn't matter. I don't have to think of anything. I just have to let his hands mold me as they wish to. I just have to let myself go, and dance, and not touch myself after, which might be the hardest part.

But that's Master's business, not Vlad's. I'm going to be Vlad's most obedient student ever. I will make my father proud, and my mentor, and my husband too, whoever he is.

8

THE NEXT MORNING, Olga is at the piano and Master is in the studio again. He's wearing another of his black suits; his dress shoes are shiny black beacons on the sprung floors, a reminder that he's here for business, not pleasure. He says nothing while Vlad takes me through the same warmup routine we do every time.

I'm still feeling energized after my conversation with my father last night, and I launch into each position with renewed intensity, hoping that Master will notice that yesterday didn't break me. I'm trying as hard as I ever have, maybe even harder, to be good for him.

Vlad doesn't seem interested in that, though. And he addresses all of his commentary on me to Master, as if I'm not even in the room. "Three weeks together and she can't even get this leg up high enough," he says, yanking my lifted leg higher in an arabesque. "And her torso has no tone to it, no frame." He flicks my sternum once, disinterestedly and barks at Olga to start from the beginning.

I feel like a broken doll they're considering tossing in the trash, and no matter how hard I work, Vlad's criticisms are constant, endless barbs. There are no tender touches today, and that almost makes it worse that I'm still craving them; every time he puts me in my place I long for a sweet little burst of pressure to take the sting out of the hurt.

It never comes, and by the time we move away from the barre, and I'm performing on autopilot, so anxious that I jump the gun on Vlad's commands more than once. We both know what he's going to say next, but that doesn't matter; I'm supposed to wait for his cue every time, to move only and exactly as he tells me to move.

The frustration and tension builds and builds, and it's even worse knowing I can't go home and touch myself after; there will be no release today, no way to turn this experience into something other than what it is, which is painful and humiliating. The wetness between my legs just feels like an admission that I'm weak and needy. Finally Vlad just makes me stop and has me stand in first position in the middle of the floor, like a beginning dancer.

"You see?" he says to Master. "She's impossible. I've tried, but I can't make anything useful out of her."

I expect Master to agree, and to dismiss me forever, and tears prick hotly at the corners of my eyes. I wanted so badly to come in and do everything right today, and instead this is the worst I've done since my first day with Vlad.

Master surprises me by regarding me quietly before saying, "She's distracted right now. Too in her head. She performs better when she's aroused, I think." He's looking at his own reflection in the mirror, straightening the already impeccable cuffs of his shirt.

Finally, he addresses me directly, and my heart leaps.

"Juliette, take your leotard off and do it again."

For a moment, I blanch and glance at Olga, who's looking right at me. What the hell? This seems like a recipe for less concentration, not more. And Master has already seen me naked, but Vlad—

But the lesson is obedience, and I'm hell-bent on learning it.

I tug off the bodysuit biting back a sigh of relief as my breasts are bared to the studio's cool air. My nipples are standing at attention, begging to be touched, and both men must know by now exactly how much I like this. Then I slip the leg warmers and panties down, leaving me helplessly naked except for my pointe shoes.

"You heard your Master," Vlad says. "You're too in your head. You need to be in your body." He circles me as he speaks, his gaze like a ribbon he's wrapping around me, soft silk that teases before it pulls tight. He reaches out and touches one shoulder, trailing his hand down my arm and raising goosebumps along the skin there. "You need to feel every part of yourself," he says. "Begin. But half time." He looks at Olga, snapping his fingers to set her metronome, and though she follows it, I can sense her disgust for me and my nudity.

We move through the rest of the routine at a torturous pace, because every time I land in a position, Vlad's hands are on me again, adjusting my hips or tugging my hair to put my head in place. With every graze, every smack, every tug, I lose further track of whether I'm dancing well or not. All I know is that I'm wet for him, and Master can tell. I'm following Vlad's commands like they're the only words I've ever heard in my life, letting him tell my body exactly what to do.

The only other thing I know is that Master is watching, and that's the hottest part of the whole thing. I want Vlad to touch me so badly, but I also want Master to knock his hands away, to claim me for himself and handle me like I belong to him. I want to win his approval, and I want to look over and see his cock hard in his pants for me. I want to impress this unimpressible being, this clockwork man with his endless stream of exacting commands, and it pushes my performance as my body begs him for even just a word of approval.

When the routine ends and I find myself standing in first position again, I'm a little startled. I'm facing Master and my own reflection in the mirror, with Vlad standing behind me. "Better," Vlad allows, which is as close to praise as I get most days.

Then he reaches around to slip a hand between my thighs, his fingers sliding along the bare seam of my pussy, giving me pressure where I need it most. My clit is already throbbing from being touched while I was dancing, from knowing that Master could see everything as I moved.

I look up and find myself pinned in place by his gaze, suspended between the wild green of his eyes and Vlad's body behind me, the strength of his arm around my waist. Vlad's hand keeps moving, slow, steady, and no one says anything. Master doesn't ask him to stop, and he doesn't tell me I can come.

The whole scene reminds me too much of what happened in my bathroom last night—riding Master's hard thigh, the way my vulnerable naked body looks in all of these mirrors, and I drop my gaze to the floor. I'm too overwhelmed by sensation, and I can't stand knowing that Master is watching me, that he's seeing me get used like this, judging whether or not I can hold back an orgasm, waiting for me to fail to obey his command again.

Vlad's hands are strong and hot against me, and if I was allowed, I would unspool in a second, come on his fingers like a whore. But I can't. I don't know how I'm going to survive this situation, only that I have to. My breath is coming in harsh, shocked little pants, the only sound other than his fingers working my wetness in the silent, still room.

I try to focus on anything else as Vlad plays with me, stringing me tauter and tauter until I know I only have a minute before I snap. I try to remember miserable experiences—frigid water on morning swims in the Baltic Sea the time we summered there, and how my feet ached last night, the smell of the stables when I mucked them out. I try to use Olga's presence in the room as a turn off, but it does nothing to block the press of tension. I'm reduced to counting the seconds, just trying to focus on the numbers, on anything that isn't what's happening in this room, between my legs, when Vlad lets me go so suddenly I almost fall to the floor. I'm dizzy and I'm still so wet, but I did it. I didn't come.

"I knew you could do it," Vlad rumbles.

I'm glowing. Finally, finally, I succeeded at something.

But then I look up from the floor and realize that Master's not here. Instead, he's left a note on the mirror. All it says is, "My office. Tomorrow, 9:23 a.m."

9

IN THE MORNING, Jane has an outfit ready for me, and I don't question it. This set is less demure than the last one was. The first time we met, Master put me in black tulle with pink flowers; today's set is a black lace bodysuit edged in black satin that reminds me of the contrast between my naked body and Master's dark suits, Vlad's black dance clothes and my pink leotards. I hope this means my training is about to advance in some way.

Either Jane picked it or Master did, but either way, I'm grateful that I don't have to try to figure out what to wear to this mysterious appointment. Will he even be there? Or is this the next step in his game, and now I'll spend weeks chasing in-person appointments instead of phone calls?

Either way, I know what I'm supposed to do. I walk into the lobby at 9:23 a.m. exactly. My heels are higher this time, the black patent pumps coming to a wicked point at the toe, and my pencil skirt is so tight that I would have worn it without underwear if that hadn't been included in the outfit, too.

The beautiful receptionist whose name I still don't know

greets me and leads me back to a new room—an office, this time, smaller and more personal than the conference room where I first met Master.

It's just as intimidating, though: the walls are lined in bookshelves filled with antique volumes, spines bound in green and stamped in gold, and in the center of the room sits an antique oak desk that looks like it weighs about as much as our yacht does. The carpet is a darker shade of green than Master's eyes, and I can make the comparison easily, because he's waiting for me there when I walk through the door.

So is another girl. She seems like she's a few years older than I am; her hair is dark where mine is light, and her body curves where I sometimes worry mine is a little too straight and flat. Most of all, though, I don't like the look she's giving me. Or, rather, the look she's not giving me: she doesn't acknowledge me when I walk through the door. Instead, her gaze is fixed steadily on Master, like he's the only other person in the room.

"Juliette," Master says. "This is Tammy."

I flip through the names of girls I've met from other families like mine, but nothing resembling Tammy comes up. Who is she? What is she doing here?

"Tammy," Master says. "Place your feet 18 inches apart. Pick your shirt up over your tits. Hands on your head. Drop to your knees."

Like a doll, she does exactly as ordered: feet apart, shirt up, hands up. Her knees hit the floor before I've finished processing what he asked for. She finally deigns to look at me, then, giving me a smug little side-eyed glance that suggests she knows I wouldn't have done it as quickly, or as gracefully.

I feel my hackles rising. I have never been bested by another student before, and I'm not going to start today.

Master pulls a tape measure out of his pocket.

"See for yourself," he says.

For a second, I think he means her, but then I realize he's holding it out to me. When I press the tape measure between her feet—which aren't bruised and bleeding from weeks of miserable ballet lessons—there is exactly eighteen inches of space between them.

"Good," Master says. We both know he isn't talking to me, and I wish fiercely and furiously that he was.

There's a clink of metal, and I look up to see Master undoing his belt buckle. I stand and watch in mesmerized silence as he unzips his fly and pulls his cock out of his pants.

His erection is enormous, and throbbing a needy red. He's bigger than anything I've ever seen or imagined, so thick I would gag on it, but I want to try anyway. Blood pounds between my legs, and even though I know it's not for me, I can't stop wanting it. My expensive new under-wear is already soaked through with the evidence of my desire.

With her hands laced on top of her head, Tammy gives me a look radiant with smug satisfaction, as Master says, "Open your mouth."

She opens wide and he feeds his cock into her throat in a single, easy motion. My clit twitches, and I'm unbearably aware of the fact that when I put this skirt on, and the lacy black lingerie underneath it, it was with tentative hope: I wanted Master to take me the way he's taking Tammy, fucking her face with calculated ruthlessness. He uses her like his toy, careless and confident, and she takes it like she was made to do it.

"This is obedience," Master says. His voice is as steady and even as when he was discussing me with Vlad yesterday, like this girl isn't trying to suck his brain out through his dick right now. "This is how it's done. Tammy here doesn't have half your advantages, but next week, she's marrying far,

far above her station to a man who's going to make her a star."

The jealousy I've been trying to restrain finally roars through me, as incandescent and explosive as a firework. This is my world. I've always been Daddy's princess and my tutors' star student. I've never had to watch someone else set the standard for me before, and I hate it more than I ever could have imagined.

"This is what we do here," Master continues, "and this is what our clients expect. I know you're going to make it, Juliette, but I don't think you believe it." Before I even have time to process what that means, he taps Tammy's ear and says, "Keep it neat for me."

I watch as his orgasm pulses out of him, and her throat works to suck down every drop. He barely reacts, looking down at her as she swallows. When he pulls out, his cock is glistening, as wet as I am for him.

"Good girl," Master says to Tammy, putting his dick away and zipping up. "You are exceptional."

She stands, beaming. I thought I was jealous when he treated Tammy's mouth like a toy worth his cock. But now, after the unequivocal praise, my envy is a hot rage in my chest.

Master, unmoved by the effect his compliment had on her, waves his hand to the door. "You can go, Tammy."

Tammy meets my gaze fully as she walks out of the room, her knees red from where she knelt on the carpet, her shirt still rucked up so her breasts are on display. Her smile is wider, now, like a cat that got into the cream; she knows she has exactly what I want, and that I have no idea how to get it for myself.

She brushes by me a little too close on the way out, and I can smell him on her: Master's scent, woodsy and earthy, that skin-close musk. She's tasted him and I'm not even allowed to come on my own fingers.

The door closes behind her with a soft *snick*, and Master and I are alone again.

"Feet 18 inches apart," he says, "and pull up your skirt."

I try to mimic Tammy's position exactly, to remember the distance between one foot and the other, as I tug my skirt up over my hips. Master's already seen me naked twice, but it still feels thrilling to have his icy eyes on my skin, taking in every inch of me. Can he tell how turned on I am right now? That I want to try to throat him so badly I can barely breathe?

He kicks my feet farther apart without a word. Then he says, "That's 18 inches. Memorize it."

I look down and try to figure out some way I'll know in the future—what makes this 18 inches and not 17.5. How do my legs feel? My feet? Where's my balance? Is this what all of that ballet was actually about? I do feel more in touch with my body than I did a month ago, more prepared for this kind of challenge, even if I'm still worried I'll fail it when the time comes to perform for real.

Master isn't interested in that, though. Instead, he reaches between my legs and pushes my panties aside to feel my cunt. I'm wet for him like I always am, my folds soaked through, so that he only has to skim his fingers there to know how badly I want more of his touch, and how much I like what he does to me. I may not deserve anything, but I want it all the same.

"I saw you yesterday with Vlad," he says. "You did well. You wanted to come, and you didn't. And now you're wet all over again. You want to suck a cock like Tammy just did, don't you?"

I nod helplessly. There's no point in pretending that I don't.

"You will," Master promises, and my heart leaps in my chest at the thought of tasting him.

Then he stands and pulls his hand away. I feel the loss keenly, an aching emptiness between my legs that pulses in time with my heartbeat. The torture of the moment is as sweet as venom; I want to keep suckling at it, even though I know it's killing me.

"But you have to let go of the conviction that it's about you." Master leans back on the desk and crosses his arms, two fingertips glistening with cunt juices. "It's not. And until you know that, you are not to come by your own hand or anyone else's. Obedience is a marathon. Not a sprint."

I don't dare move, not even to nod. He'll tell me what he wants next from me. My only job is to wait. I will be better at this than Tammy was; one day, she'll see me and I'll be able to smile smugly at her, and put her back in her place.

"Now you can drop your skirt," Master says, and I can't pretend I'm not disappointed. I know he won't give me anything else, and if he did touch me I don't know how I could contain myself; I would come whether I wanted to or not. It's almost a kindness.

But still, I hate to leave his presence. Here, at least, I have a purpose. I'm learning. And I love the way it feels to be with him: how he challenges me in ways no one else ever has. Makes me feel things I had never dared to imagine for myself.

"Go home," he says. "Tomorrow will be your recital. My Client will be there."

Oh my God. Is this really happening?

10

——————

DADDY'S GONE TONIGHT, so Jane gives Eloise the night off and makes us dinner, which we eat together in the kitchen. I changed when I got home, put on my silk pajamas and plain cotton underwear, but I'm still uncomfortably turned on; I can't find a way to sit that doesn't remind me how badly I want to be able to thumb at my clit right now, fuck myself on my fingers until I'm shuddering with release.

Jane notices my edginess. "Can I help?" she asks. She's made a simple meal for us tonight, salmon steaks seared with lemon and fresh herbs, served alongside a green salad and fresh bread with butter. I take a slice from the loaf, noting its crisp crust and soft, doughy interior; I slather it thick with butter before taking a bite. This is the only indulgence I'm allowed, and I will take advantage of it. I want Master on my tongue and down my throat; instead, I leave teeth marks in the butter, evidence of my appetites.

"You can't," I say when I've chewed and swallowed. "No one can." Okay, I'm being a bit dramatic, but really—I've been tortured and tormented for weeks now, and as far as I can tell, I'm no closer to meeting my husband than I ever was. In fact, I'm set further back, since I'm not allowed to come whenever I want. I'm allowed to be a little out of sorts.

Jane pokes another slice of bread in my direction, and I butter it just as thickly. "It's just that Master made a rule for me, after the other night," I say. "Since I couldn't come when he told me to, now I'm not allowed to touch myself at all until he says so. The other day at the studio Vlad touched me...everywhere...and I just had to keep myself from coming. And then I saw Master today, and he touched me, too, though not for as long. I'm so turned on I could die. All the time. And I have no idea when that will change."

Jane nods slowly. "I know how you feel," she says.

"Do you?"

"The other night—I lied to you. I didn't just hear Master spanking you from my room. When I left, I was curious what he would do. And I wanted to make sure you were okay," she adds.

"It's fine," I tell her. "I'm not mad. I understand."

"So I stood under your window. That's how I—how I knew what I knew."

"And then what happened?" Did Master give Jane some kind of command, too? I know he doesn't belong to me; he isn't even my husband. But still, I can't help being a little jealous.

"Bruce caught me," Jane says.

"Oh!" Our head caretaker is handsome and well-muscled, with sun-lightened hair and hands tough with calluses; I've seen him split firewood and watched the muscles in his shoulders work with helpless fascination. But he's also exacting and demanding—running the staff with an iron fist, and catching Jane eavesdropping might not have ended well for her. "I can have Daddy talk to him."

"No, it's not..." Jane is blushing, but she doesn't need any encouragement. "He said if I liked spankings so much, I had earned one of my own."

Bruce isn't as big as Master, but he's plenty strong, and I'm sure his smacks stung almost as bad. My bottom winces in sympathy as Jane continues. "He took me to the filthy work shed and put me over his knee. His hands—they were so big. He felt so big underneath me, all over."

Jane finally looks up from her plate, where she's mostly been pushing her food around, and we share a sympathetic look. We've known each other a long time, and I know exactly what she's feeling right now: desire and shame, need and want. The heat of the memory of being overwhelmed by someone, taken without mercy—all while still being fully clothed.

"After," Jane continues. "He said he'd call on me again if I was naughty. Then he just dismissed me."

"Did you just leave?"

"What else could I do. He's—he's so powerful. I feel like I'm going to die of wanting him. Every time I see him on the grounds now I want to rub myself against him like a cat in heat."

Jane's shame has melted away, and the flush on her face looks like pleasure instead of embarrassment. She even looks like she's glowing a little bit, lit up from within by the excitement of this experience.

"It's torture," I say.

"It is," she agrees. "But he barely acknowledges me, and at the same time, I know he sees me. The thing is, I know what I have to do it be 'naughty.' Just pick a flower or something, right, but I want to be good, you know?"

Now it's my turn to look down at my plate. I've somehow managed to eat most of my food while she talked, mesmerized by her perspective on this experience. Jane's gone through so much of what I have in the last few weeks, but instead of being sulky and sad, the way I've been, she seems to be enjoying it. Wanting more, even. Not only that, she's had to deal with my sulkiness and sadness *while* learning to discipline her own body for Bruce.

"It doesn't bother you?" I ask. "To not…"

I don't even know how to finish that sentence. Have whatever you want? Jane has never had that; in a way, neither have I. And as much as I want the end to all of these rules and restrictions, I also know that that would mean the end of my relationship with Master, and I'm not ready for that yet, either. I'm not ready to be done with the way it feels to submit to him, to just give myself over to exactly what he wants from me, and somehow I know Jane feels the same… yet she's acting as if it's pleasure, not a burden.

I get up to refill our water glasses to give myself time to think through all of this. I've been acting like this whole situation was a burden, just something my husband cooked up to torment me, an impossible set of tests I'll never pass. But it's also a privilege. Master and Vlad, all those men in the studio the other day, even the receptionist who has to pass messages between Master and me—they're all giving me their time and attention. And it's not like this is for nothing. I am learning to please my husband, just not in the ways I used to expect.

Plus, it's not like I hate it *all the time*.

"Do you think I've been ungrateful?" I ask Jane when I return to the table. "I know I've been complaining a lot, these last few weeks. I never thought you might be going through something similar."

Thank God, Jane laughs. "I've known you for most of your life, Juliette," she reminds me. "I know how hard you work. From the way you talk about it, Master hasn't gone easy on you, and neither has Vlad." She gives me a meaningful look. "I've seen those bruises and blisters on your feet," she reminds me. "I know."

"Yes, but—"

"But nothing. You thought you'd be married by now. You're being made to wait. Anyone would be anxious and jittery. I know I am."

"Thank you," I say, bowing my head. "For dinner, and for your friendship."

"Of course," Jane says simply.

THE CONVERSATION with Jane distracts me for a while, but when I go back to my room, I get out a tape measure and mark eighteen inches on my floor in chalk, and spend an hour trying to get my body to memorize its shape. I get better, closer, but I'm no Tammy—by the time I know I have to go to bed so I'll be well-rested for tomorrow's recital, I'm still regularly missing it by a half an inch or more. Hopefully Master won't insist on a pop quiz on it tomorrow.

It also means that Master fills my thoughts as I go through my nighttime routine, and when I'm lying in bed in the dark, I'm so desperate to be touched—by him, or myself —that I think I'll never fall asleep. I keep remembering the time he came to me, just appeared in my room, and spanked me until I cried out. The other night, when he let me press myself against him and use his body for my pleasure.

I manage to keep my hands to myself, but when I finally fall asleep, my dreams are feverish with want.

I'm in the back of a limo, naked, with Bruce and Jane. "You can do it, Juliette," Jane is saying. "Just concentrate."

"Be a good girl," Bruce says, but he's not looking at me; his gaze is fixed on Jane.

The limo dissolves around me, and before I'm ready I'm there: in the studio, not even wearing my pointe shoes, while a mass of men in black suits watch me. I know Vlad and

Master are among them, but I can't find their faces in the crowd, and then Olga starts playing, and I have to dance.

My hands are tied behind my back with a set of pink ribbons, which makes it particularly hard to balance, but I flow through the movements, almost melting into them, letting the long weeks of training take me over. As I move, though, a man separates himself from the rest and walks over to me, running his hands along my leg as I lift it into an arabesque. He subsides, and another one takes his place, touching my shoulder, my arm, my bound hands. One of the men is always touching me, but it's never the same man twice, and never where I want them—at the aching tips of my nipples and at the hollow center of need between my legs.

They stroke me and tease me, whispering filth into my ear when they do. "Everyone here can see your cunt," one reminds me.

"We're all hard for your whore mouth," another one says.

"You're so wet I could just slip right in," a third notes, and I can't contain my shudder of want.

Finally, Vlad materializes; he has his cane again, and without him having to ask, I know to bend over, the ribbons slipping from around my wrists so that I can brace myself against the mirror.

Then I get to watch my own face—my open mouth and blow-wide pupils—as he spanks me, each blow singing through me. The cane looks heavy but each smack transmits white-hot pleasure, the sting subsumed by the pulsing in my pussy. He spanks me in a ruthless rhythm, my hips rising to meet each thrust. I know I can't come, even in the dream, but I want to. I want to so badly.

"At least you know how to do this well," Vlad says. The spanking stops, and I let out a small cry when he pushes the cane inside me. I want more. I need—*more*.

Vlad grabs my hair, tugging my head so that I'm looking up from my own reflection in the mirror.

"Look," he says. "He's watching you get fucked."

And then, finally, I see him: Master, with his cock out like it was for Tammy, the hot thick length of him in his powerful hand as he watches me and strokes himself. My body feels like water; I want to lap at him everywhere.

"You can't come yet," Master says. "But I'm going to, Juliette. Keep still for me while I come on your ass."

"Please," I beg. "Please, please—"

I don't know what I'm pleading for, only that I am.

I wake up in the morning sweat-soaked and hazy, so wet I'm surprised I haven't soaked my sheets, but I know I kept my promise: even in the dream, I managed not to come.

11

_____

SINCE I DIDN'T SLEEP WELL, I was worried that by the time the recital rolled around, I would be a wreck, but instead I'm strangely calm. I've finally passed at least one of Master's tests, and then another last night, even if he didn't know it. It would have been easy to thumb at my clit for just a few seconds when I woke up this morning; I was so close it would have taken almost nothing to push me over the edge. But I didn't. I waited.

I'm waiting still when the car pulls up at the house where the recital will take place. It's one of the older places in town, a mansion built when craftsmen took pride in every detail of their work. The façade's white stone catches the sunset's last rays and glows a soft, sweet pink; the fountain in the driveway is lit up and glowing, and the enormous lawn is a lush, brilliant emerald even in the early dusk. I feel almost beautiful again as I step out of the car, wearing a simple wrap dress with my dance clothes in my bag. This house was built for a princess to live in. Maybe tonight I'll earn myself a title.

Or at least an orgasm.

Jane wasn't allowed to accompany me, so I'm alone in the

driveway when a sharp woman in her forties approaches and ushers me into the house. Our heels clack and echo through grand rooms, each one high-ceilinged and beautiful, with white stone archways and stained glass windows, until we come to the house's theater.

This space is classic and glamorous, paneled in dark wood, with plush red velvet seats and a red velvet curtain held in place by gold-tasseled ties.

"There's a room backstage for you to change and warm up," the woman says with a smile so professional, it's almost warm. I wonder if she's shocked at what I'm here to do—or maybe she doesn't even know, and why I care is a mystery to me until she turns around and I notice the twist of her bun.

A shot of memory runs through me.

My mother coiled her bun like that.

My mother who I loved, and who died was part of the same world I'm part of. She probably had the same training I'm going through right now, and the same kind of marriage with my father that I'm about to have.

I know for sure that she'd be proud of me. I'm a woman now; my husband will be here tonight, and if I do well, it will show him how well suited we are. How happy we can be together, like my own parents were.

I go backstage to dress and warm up. Tonight I barely even feel my blisters; I just concentrate on each muscle as I move, preparing my whole body for what's to come.

It turns out I'm not the only act on the bill tonight; a troupe of dancers joins me after a while, murmuring to each other in Russian that I can't understand and don't speak. They perform first, an elegant modern number that makes the most of their lithe bodies and strong limbs. I watch them from backstage, peering around the curtains, and even though I try to concentrate on the dance and not worry about the audience, I can't help scanning for him. The Client. My husband.

The audience is all male—fifty or so men in sharply cut suits who sit straight and attentive. I wonder if some of them are here for some of the girls, if they're after love or merely a night of pleasure. As I scan their faces, I try to imagine how I'll know him when I see him—what I'm hoping to recognize in his face, but I can't figure it out. All I know is how I want him to feel. I want him to be handsome, of course, and powerful, like Master. I feel certain that when our eyes meet, I will know the man I was meant for.

But their performance ends, and I still haven't figured it out. My earlier calm deserts me as I take the stage; for several long moments, my heart is in my throat, and I wonder if I'll be able to perform at all.

Then I take hold of myself. I am Juliette Newmont, my father's only and most beloved daughter, star student in every one of my endeavors. Whether I recognize him or not, my husband is here, and I will not disappoint him. I will be perfectly, flawlessly obedient for him.

The music starts up, and I let myself melt into it. I can almost hear Vlad murmuring each move into my ear, and I obey him instantly, my body taking the shapes his hands have described each day for weeks. The rigor he taught me turns to pleasure; a flush rises all over me as I move, half from physical exertion and half from the sheer simple pleasure of knowing that I'm doing exactly what he wants me to do, what Master wants me to do, what the Client wants me to do.

The world seems to melt away as I give myself over to the movement, and for the first time, I truly understand what my husband is offering me in exchange for my obedience. If it's this feeling, it's worth it.

Afterwards, it feels like I float off the stage, still as light and easy as air. The Russian girls are gone, and it's just Vlad waiting for me in the dressing room, out of his practice clothes but still clad in customary all black.

"That," he says, "was magnificent. That was the performance I've been trying to get out of you all along."

I know I did well, but having Vlad confirm it gives me an extra glow of satisfaction. He's been the most impossible critic I've ever worked with, so I know he wouldn't say it if my performance hadn't been extraordinary.

"You let yourself go finally," he says. "Felt, instead of thought. It was beautiful to watch, Juliette. You did exactly what you were supposed to do."

"Thank you," I say. "For everything. I couldn't have done it without you."

Vlad grins at me. He knows.

Then he takes my hands in his, a gentle touch unlike any of the ones we've shared before. "It's been a pleasure working with you," he says. "But it's time for us to say goodbye. Our time together has come to an end."

It has? For weeks I've fantasized about the day I never had to see this hateful man again, so I'm surprised to find myself hurt by this news. I just figured out how to give Vlad what he wants; I was looking forward to coming in tomorrow and doing it again. "Oh," I hear myself say.

"This part of your training is over," Vlad continues. "Be proud of yourself, Juliette. You did well."

"Will I see you again?"

He gives a philosophical shrug. "Who can say?"

I surprise myself again by bursting out with, "I'll miss you." I will, too. Not just the way his hands felt on my body, though of course I will miss that, but the certainty I had with him. I may not have always liked it, but I understood our routine. Now I have no idea what happens next.

Vlad nods. "Be who you are and you won't miss a thing,"

he says. Then he leans in and kisses me once, tenderly, on my cheek. He reaches into his pocket and hands me an envelope before he turns to leave.

Alone in the practice room, still sweaty and breathless from my performance, I look at the envelope and remember the one that my father held on the deck of our yacht. It feels like a lifetime ago that I was that innocent girl in her sundress, daydreaming about my house in the Maldives, thinking she was about to meet her husband, that her life was about to change.

Well, it has changed, just not in the ways I expected. I've changed, and I'm not sure how I feel about that yet.

But I do know what I want to do next.

I open the envelope and find a note inside, written in what is by now Master's familiar handwriting. "Wear what's in the bag," it says. "Blouse fully buttoned, panties down two inches below your crotch."

I'm giving the room a panicked once-over, looking for a bag, when there's a knock at the door; I open it to find a shopping bag sitting on the floor, its handle tied neatly with a pink satin bow. Inside there's a cream silk blouse, a set of apricot-colored lingerie, and another pencil skirt like the one Master outfitted me in when I came to his office and met Tammy.

I try not to get ahead of myself, but I can't help the way my pulse picks up when I think of that encounter. He promised me I would be allowed to suck him—is that my reward tonight? I imagine his fingers slipping under my skirt and finding me bare, touching me again—I have to stop thinking about it, though, because I'm already wet, and I'm still not allowed to come until he says.

I dress myself quickly, wishing I had been able to take a shower, that I had more than touchup makeup with me so I could make sure I looked exactly right for him.

Then I scan down the rest of the note, and realize that there's one more instruction. I'm supposed to wear this to a restaurant on the other side of town in exactly thirty-two minutes.

Fuck.

I run.

12

THE SPARROW'S Nest isn't the hippest spot in town; instead, it's a well-kept secret that caters to the city's elite. I've only been here once before, at a business dinner with Daddy when I was sixteen. He brought me along in order to educate me as well as to test me—to make sure I knew how to charm the men at the table and use the right fork, as well as to get used to the kinds of duties I'd have to assume once I was someone's wife.

That night I was so nervous that I barely tasted the spoonfuls of caviar on perfectly fluffy blini paired with shots of icy vodka; a decadent lobster risotto followed by an impossibly delicate series of tiny pastries, each one topped with jewel-like pieces of sugared fruit. The Sparrow's Nest is where serious business happens, but it's also where you enjoy the fruits of your victories, and a possibility I haven't allowed myself to contemplate fills my head: am I about to meet my husband? Now, with my hair still in its ballet bun and my panties halfway off, my pussy bare underneath the tight material of my skirt?

I pause for a moment before I go to speak to the hostess, taking the room in: the floor-to-ceiling windows, which give a view of the city twinkling below us; the black tufted leather of the barstools and chairs and the elegant, beautiful people sitting in them. The room is bustling tonight; The Sparrow's Nest is never an easy reservation, and I wonder how far in advance my husband booked us this dinner. I wonder if he believed in me all this time.

I set my shoulders back. This is how the rest of my life begins.

But when the hostess leads me to my table, set almost exactly in the center of the room, it isn't some stranger waiting for me. Instead it's Master standing by his chair, waiting like a perfect gentleman. I notice more than a few of the women in the room eyeing him, and then eyeing me as I approach. As ever, he is immaculately self-contained—quite aware of, yet supremely indifferent to everything around him.

"Hello, Master," I say once the hostess has left us alone.

"Sit," he instructs me, pulling out my chair. He pushes it in as I sit, then takes his own seat across from me.

There are no menus on the table, but after a few moments, a waiter arrives bearing a bowl of soup and a glass of white wine.

I nod my thanks to him, but don't touch either, waiting for Master's instructions.

"Eat," he says. "And don't spill a drop." He doesn't sound particularly pleased with me, but he doesn't sound disappointed, either.

I take a delicate spoonful and lift it carefully to my lips, anxious to do as I've been told. The broth is beautifully flavored, rich and complex with umami I almost but don't quite recognize; I close my eyes at the pleasure of it.

"Vlad gave you high marks," Master says.

I take another careful spoonful of soup, waiting to see if I'm supposed to keep listening, or if I'm allowed to respond.

"You may speak," Master says.

"I enjoyed working with him," I say. "I didn't necessarily want to be a better dancer, really? Until I just did what he told me, and I got so much better. Then I was so proud of it. It's like obedience is its own reward."

Master nods. "You learned a lot," he says. "Drink some wine."

I do as instructed. The white is minerally but not astringent, a perfect complement to the soup. Whoever ordered this meal—Master or the Client—took care with it.

As I set my glass down, I feel Master's foot under the table, nudging at the inside of one of my ankles.

"Eighteen inches," he says.

Shit. I wish I'd thought to practice sitting, but I do my level best to put my feet where they're supposed to be.

"Good enough," he says.

Good enough isn't good enough for me though. Not anymore. I want to be perfect.

And then I want to be with him, whoever he ends up being.

"Can I ask a question?"

Master nods. "You may."

"Is he coming? Here? Tonight?"

"He? You mean my Client?" He tsks. "No."

I fiddle with my soup spoon for a moment, trying to keep my face down so he won't see the disappointment that must be written all over it. Was that always the plan, or is he avoiding me because he doesn't want me anymore? Did I succeed at this test, but fail at the whole project of obedience?

"What did he think?" I ask.

"Stop playing with your soup."

I put the spoon down and take another sip of wine, trying to gin up my confidence to ask a question I both do and do not want to know the answer to. "Is he still interested?"

"He was pleased."

Relief floods my body, as sweet and hot as anything I've felt in the last month. I'm so glad and grateful I could cry. "Really?" I ask.

"Really. He said you earned an orgasm." Master's tone doesn't change at all when he says, "Would you like that?"

There's only one answer. "Yes."

Master assesses me, and for the first time I think he's pleased with me—with my honesty, and with what he's about to do to me.

"Well then. Come," he says, his voice languid and silky, a rumble that strokes me as surely as his fingers did in his office the other day. The orgasm that's been building for days, since Vlad touched me in the ballet studio, since last night's sweat-soaked dream, since Master's fingers dipped inside of me, rips through me like a rocket, and all the self-control in the world can't keep me from shuddering and crying out as my pussy quivers and my thighs shake with the aftershocks.

When I open my eyes, every single person in the restaurant is looking at me.

I lift my glass in apology. "The wine's really good," I say.

Someone chuckles, and when I look across the table, I realize it's Master, his face creased into an easy, natural smile. I've never seen him express any amusement before. He's always beautiful, but even more so like this, and I know from now on I'll be greedy for more glimpses of this side of him.

It feels like the orgasm has relaxed us both, so I decide to try to get just a tiny bit of information out of him. "When will I meet my husband?" I ask.

"Why are you so eager?" he returns.

"I can't stand all this waiting. It's making me crazy."

He raises one eyebrow. "Funny you should mention that. Your next lesson—"

Oh my God. "There are more lessons?"

"You clearly need them."

Oh God, oh God, oh God. I barely made it through this one. What does my husband expect of me? How can I be sure I'll achieve it?

"How many more are there?" I ask.

Master reaches into the breast pocket of his suit and pulls out a small envelope. To think, twenty minutes ago I was hoping I'd be done with those. "You'll find out once you learn patience."

He puts the envelope on the table between us and stands with his soup untouched.

"You can open it when you're done eating," he says, and then he leaves.

I watch the crowd watch him go, his body making waves in the room, rippling through it like the current across a body of water. Maybe I'll eat everything on the menu, I think, have a nice long leisurely dinner all by myself after all my hard work. I could stay here all night, wasting time.

But it doesn't actually appeal to me; I can't stop thinking about what might happen next, and I've totally lost my appetite. I push the soup and wine away from me and grab the envelope, ripping it open to get at whatever's inside.

The note simply reads:

Lesson 2 - Patience
Agency M: Tomorrow. 12:01pm

"Fuck!"

Everyone's looking at me again, but that doesn't matter.

Let them look. I'm leaving anyway. I stand up and walk out, unbearably aware of how wet I am from my orgasm. The placement of my underwear two inches below my crotch, is a constant reminder of who's in charge of me now, and that I still don't even know his name.

TEMPT

My first lesson hurt.
But not as much as M's judgement.
Now he calls me impatient.
My second lesson strips me bare, outside and in.
What a pretty picture I must make.
But I'm tired of waiting...

1

STANDING on the carpet in Master's office, I make sure my Jimmy Choo's are exactly eighteen inches apart. I'm wearing the outfit he picked out for me, even though it required another late-night shopping trip—my companion, Jane, had to call the boutique and get them to re-open when we got his instructions, since I didn't have this particular silk jacquard Chloe dress in my closet. So I can't help being pleased with myself—it's barely been a month since the first time I stepped foot in here, but this time, I know to stand still and wait for him to tell me what to do next...no matter how long it takes.

It's Master's role to shape me into the kind of wife my husband deserves. I still haven't met the man I'm going to marry, but I've been promised to him since childhood, and apparently, he has very specific thoughts about his future wife's abilities—so much so that he's demanded that I go through strict erotic finishing before we even meet.

I'm still getting used to all that this course entails. I am an excellent student, but my childhood tutoring was far more traditional, things like horseback riding, coding, and learning

Latin, Greek, and the romance languages. I spent my
summers swimming laps in the ocean and I've sat front row
at haute couture fashion shows, but this is the first time I've
had my lingerie customized for me and my orgasms delayed
or denied at the whims of a Master.

But I also find that the more I explore this life, the more I
like it. I especially like when Master walks in and looks at me
like he is right now, all of his cold, severe control directed at
my body in its thin ruffled dress, a stark contrast to his large,
strong body, tucked into his usual impeccably tailored dark
suit.

Apparently deciding I've demonstrated my obedience
well enough for one morning, he finally gets up from where
he's been lounging behind his desk and hands me an envelope made of thick white cardstock. It looks just like the one
that first directed me to this office, as well as the one that
sent me to the legendary Bogatsvo Dance Studio for ballet
lessons that were equal parts about my dancing and my
ability to concentrate when a gorgeous man had his hand
between my legs.

"You may open it," Master says.

I'm too excited to be careful, tugging the envelope open
so forcefully that the paper rips a little bit. I expect a repri-
mand from Master for a lack of self-control, but it doesn't
come. Inside, the card reads: *The Studio of Antoine Dupont,
Wednesday, 10:23 a.m.*

There's an address on the coast beneath it.

I recognized the Bogatsvo by its reputation, but I've never
heard of Antoine Dupont. Whoever he is, though, I'm sure
he's just as highly regarded as my last instructor, Vlad, was.
My husband may be willing to let other men touch me before
he does, but he has the resources to ensure that they're only
the best in their fields. Of course they are, though: in the
circles we run in, the best is expected. Our families are as

wealthy and secretive as you can imagine. The point of our marriage is to create an alliance between them and knit our world even more closely together, shoring up his power, and also my own.

If it ever happens, that is.

I have a zillion questions, and when I look at Master, he can see it on my face. It warms something inside of me to know that he can read me now—that he wants to be able to respond to me at least a little bit, since I'm so desperate to respond to him. I've never met a man as forceful. Or as handsome.

He nods, encouraging me to speak.

"Who sets up my appointments with these guys?" I ask. "Do you like...use them all the time, for all the girls?"

Master shakes his head just slightly. "The client's chosen them specifically for you."

I can't help myself; I try pushing him just a little bit, mostly to see what he'll let me get away with since I've already been so good for him. "By client, you mean my husband to be. Who's that, again?"

Master is in a good mood; he smirks at me, the side of his beautiful mouth tilting up as he shakes his head again, more surely this time.

"You can wear what you have on now."

That's it. He's not going to give me a name until he's good and ready, and I wish that knowledge didn't make me wet for him every time. I know he can see my nipples, stiff under my dress, begging for his huge hands to touch them. But my breasts are not his. They belong to a man I've never met.

"His technique can be uncomfortable, but it works. You're to obey Antoine the same way you'd obey me, and the way you will obey your husband—without complaint." He sits behind his desk and opens a folder as if I'm not even there.

I can take a hint. The conversation is over.

ANTOINE DUPONT'S studio is in a beautiful old building a few miles north of us along the coast. It's been gorgeously restored, so that the place feels both weathered and modern; it smells like sea air, and the light in every room I see is so pure and clear that I'm not surprised when Antoine turns out to be a painter.

His housekeeper ushers me to his top-floor studio, where he's waiting for me. My last instructor, Vlad, had a dancer's body, strong and compact; he looked like an anatomical diagram in his leotards and leggings. Antoine, on the other hand, is no less gorgeous, but tall and rangy, with an artist's long fingers and a mop of dark, unruly curls. His clothes are covered in paint, and he assesses me openly, taking me in from the top of my blonde head to my perfectly pedicured toes, which are currently crammed into the Jimmy Choos, as instructed.

I must look good enough, because Antoine steps forward and kisses me on each cheek. "Juliette," he murmurs, his French accent softening my name into something that makes my knees feel a little weak. "*Enchanté.*"

"*Tout le plaisir est pour moi,*" I reply. French is one of the languages I speak fluently, though I'm having trouble remembering my words right now, so I sincerely hope that most of our conversation will be in English.

"I wasn't sure if you were familiar with my work," he says. "So I have some of my recent canvases out. Take a look. I need you to understand what we are here to do together."

Okay. Great. I can look at art. I once spent eight months in the Louvre, learning to identify painters and styles on sight, and even to do some of my own sketching. So far, this is way easier than my last assignment.

That is, until I realize what's on those canvases. Each one

contains a nude woman's body, faceless, in a sexual pose. They're beautifully rendered, with an almost photorealistic technique: I can see goosebumps on the inside of a caramel-colored thigh, and the faint impression of a bruise on the ample curve of another's ass.

It's the cunts I really can't get over, though: Antoine must spend hours between these women's legs, rendering them in minute, stunning detail. They all look like perfectly ripe fruit, sweet and wet for him, and I already know I'm going to be as weak for Antoine as I was for Vlad. I'm glad my back is to him, my face close to the painting, when a shudder ripples through me as I imagine him parting my folds, his fingers gentle but firm where I'm yielding and tender.

"These must take hours," I breathe. "I can't even begin to—"

"No," Antoine says crisply. "You cannot imagine. So, we will begin to work now. Take off your clothes and sit here." He gestures to a simple pedestal draped in a piece of white sheeting at the center of the room.

Until recently, no one aside from Jane and a few shopgirls had seen me naked; but since Master and Vlad put their eyes on me, I'm more used to undressing in front of strange men, though my hands still shake slightly as I pull down my zipper and step out of my dress, pausing briefly before peeling off my panties and bra. I make a neat pile of my clothes—the peach silk lingerie I picked out so carefully this morning is apparently an afterthought to this man—and take my place on the pedestal. I'm glad that I already saw how those other women responded to being Antoine's muse, their nipples stiff, pussies gleaming. It makes it less embarrassing to know he can see that I'm already turned on.

His frank, disinterested appraisal of my body continues through the afternoon. He treats me like another object in a still life, reminding me of what I've already experienced:

Vlad's hands on me as he corrected my posture, Master letting me ride his thigh to shuddering orgasm. Once I sit down, Antoine touches me just as rudely: spreads my legs so far apart I gasp, uses my hair to guide my head back so that the light hits my neck at a particular angle. Then he goes to go sketch for a while, leaving me breathless, straining to hold myself exactly as he wants me, the ghost of his touch taunting me the whole time.

Maybe an hour later, I'm bored out of my mind when he comes back and pinches my nipples, the stimulation making my pussy twitch with need. I gasp and recoil from the shock of it.

"Were my methods explained to you or *non?*" he asks casually, and my first reaction is to go with *non*, but that wouldn't be one hundred percent true.

His technique can be uncomfortable.

Understatement of the century.

You're to obey Antoine the same way you'd obey me.

"*Oui*," I say. "It was explained. Just not described."

He crouches down to me. "The model must lose their identity to me. You must have no thoughts of your own, and become my object." He takes one knee and spreads it towards where the light is coming in through the south-facing windows. "You are stillness and action at the same time, and this is how it's done." With a quick hand, he flicks my clit once and stands over me as the throbbing sexual energy rattles my nerves. "Exactly. Now we have it."

He walks over to his easel and sketches. I'm soaking wet again, and trembling with the effort of holding still.

I feel like I've been listening to the scratch of his pencil forever. He's flipped his sketchbook a dozen times. I want this to be over with.

"How much longer?" I ask when I can't bear another minute.

Antoine puts down his sketch pad and walks over to me with an irritated light in his eyes this time. "You're an interesting subject," he says. "But not if you can't sit still."

"I can."

"I am done." He turns his back to me. "You can go. I'll call your agent if I can work with you."

————

INSTEAD OF HEADING home when I leave, I have my driver take me back to Master's. I've never shown up at his office unannounced before, but I've never been this irritated before, either. Antoine is a masterful artist—I'm not blind—but that was a waste of a day, especially if he hasn't even decided if he wants to work with me yet. Isn't it his job to be my tutor? Which means he's supposed to teach me something. I showed up ready to learn; he was the one who ignored me for hours, refused to tell me what he wanted and then had the audacity to be angry with me when I couldn't provide. *I'll call your agent* if *I can work with you*. Since when is there an *if*?

The receptionist is sitting at the front desk when I walk in, and suddenly I'm aware that my dress is wrinkled from sitting in a pile on the floor all day, and that my makeup isn't nearly as fresh as it was in the morning. Maybe I should go home now and talk to Master later, when I'm calmer? I don't want to upset the balance between us or get myself back in trouble again, especially after the difficulties with my first tutor—when I was still figuring out how to behave.

But then I feel the ghost of Antoine's hands on me, and his distant, dismissive gaze, and I don't want to cool off. I want an answer; I want to know why the man Master hired is acting like I was supposed to make a good impression on him today, instead of the other way around.

"I'm here to see my Master," I say, flushing slightly. I never call him that in front of anyone else except for Jane. I'm embarrassed by how it sounds, small and anxious, in this luxuriously decorated room; I'm embarrassed by how much I like claiming him, even though he isn't mine.

"He can't see you," the receptionist says.

"Can I wait?" I ask.

"No."

Fuck.

A thought occurs to me. "Can I make an appointment for tomorrow?"

"Sure." The receptionist nods and pages through his schedule. I wish I could see what was on there—I'm dying to know what he's doing when he's not working with me. Is every after-work appointment a date? I can't imagine Master on a *date* with someone.

"Tomorrow, 8:54 a.m.," the receptionist says, looking up from the book with an emotionless blink of her long lashes. It's not a question or a negotiation; when I'm given a time, that's the time I will arrive.

"Thank you," I say.

I pause for a moment, just lingering, in hopes he'll walk out from the back and see me. Maybe give me a smile and an unplanned moment to talk. But no one comes, and I make myself leave before the receptionist starts to ask why I'm waiting around for a man I already made an appointment with, as if I'm entitled to his time.

2

THE ROLEX on my wrist is a precision-engineered piece of technology, a marvel of human achievement, marking time evenly and perfectly whether I'm looking at it or not.

That doesn't stop me from tapping the crystal impatiently every thirty seconds, hoping it will tell me something other than what I already know, which is that my driver is running late.

And Master hates it when I'm late. He spent weeks training me to call him at exact times—if the phone rang at 12:09 instead of 12:10, he would ignore me for a few days before letting me try again. The receptionist said 8:54 a.m., and if I'm thirty seconds early or late, who knows if he'll even let me make another appointment.

I hear footsteps behind me and turn around to see my father striding down the driveway, impeccably turned out and in no hurry whatsoever. Before I can ask where my car is, he gives me an appraising look. "I hope you'll make it to dinner tonight," he says. "Unlike last night."

"That wasn't my fault," I remind him. "I had a long day at the studio."

"Oh, right. How did it go?"

I shrug, trying to mask my irritation at everything—my own lateness, and my father's casual question. It should have gone perfectly. Instead, I don't even know if I'm going to be invited back. Much less if I want to be.

"I don't know," I tell him. "It wasn't my favorite. I'm on my way to see Master—I think I'd like to find out what else he has lined up. See if we can try something different."

Hearing this, my father stops short. "Juliette," he says. "That's not how it works."

Yes, but I don't know that, because no one's explained how it does *work,* I think, and don't say. Clearly, I'm already in enough trouble for one morning.

"You only get one shot with each of them," Daddy says. His voice is kind but his words are unyielding, and my chest goes tight with fear. "If you fail with Antoine, you fail out of the program, and then..." He doesn't finish. It's like the consequences are too much to put into words.

There's a long, stark silence.

"If that's on the horizon, tell me now," he continues. "We can make plans, of course, but it will be difficult, if you're going to be..." He pauses, and when he says the word, it's clear that it's distasteful to him. "Single."

"No!" I assure him. "No, no, I'm just being grouchy—I didn't sleep well last night. I'm on my way to Master's to figure out a few details, but everything's going to be fine. You'll be walking me down the aisle before you know it." I hope so, anyway. I've never imagined a future for myself other than the one I was promised. I don't want to. I like my life. And I'll like it more when there's a rich husband in it.

A car pulls into the driveway—but it's not the black town car I was expecting, with my regular driver, Rowan, behind the wheel. Instead, it's a bright red Alfa Romeo, piloted by a woman just as tiny and sexy as the sports car. Her hair is held back by a scarf but her cleavage is on full display as she toots the horn once, already impatient.

Daddy nods at me. "You should find a way to enjoy it," he says, "since he's going to pay top dollar for it." He gives me a little wink before starting towards the car.

"Wait a minute, who is *he*? Who's paying? How do you know?"

But Daddy's already tuned in on his girlfriend. He gets into the car and slams the door behind him, leaving me alone with more questions than ever. Does my father know what kind of painting Antoine does? Is he going to *see* my nude portrait when it goes up for sale? God, I hope not. It's one thing to be wanton in front of these strange men; it would be so different for my family to know what I'm being turned into and how many men have watched the transformation.

But something else occurs to me. Whoever buys the painting, I can find out who they are. And if it's my husband, then I'll know who *he* is.

The more I think about it, the more it makes sense. Who else would pay top dollar? Who else would be allowed to? I may not have met my husband, but he doesn't seem like the type who would let a sexual portrait of his wife, her bare cunt on prominent display, hang in anyone else's home.

Which means the faster we get this done, the faster I get to meet the man behind all of this, the man I'm going to spend my life with.

And the faster I can fuck him, after all of this torturous waiting.

That is, assuming I can convince Master to convince Antoine to take me back as a client. That's a lot of convincing.

Impatience thrums in time with my pulse. I check my watch again, and consider how badly it would mess up my feet to just walk to the studio. At a party, I can stand in heels for hours, but asphalt won't be kind to the shoes or my body, and I'm still recovering from everything Vlad and my pointe shoes put me through. Luckily, my car pulls up before I can do anything too impulsive.

"Hurry," I tell the driver. "I have places to be." And he pulls out onto the street as quickly as he can.

THE RECEPTIONIST IS on the phone when I stride into Master's office building, exactly on time, thank God. I ran every step of the way from the car to the front door. She gives me a tight little nod when she sees me, but doesn't pause her conversation, so I take a seat in one of the chairs opposite her desk, crossing my legs demurely at the ankle. I've done my part; now I just have to wait for her to announce me so I can talk to Master and explain what's going on. I'll tell him I didn't know that Antoine was my only option; I'll ask him what I need to do to ensure that he wants to paint me.

But she keeps talking, and talking, and talking, and I have to watch the minutes tick by on my watch, which I've never hated more than I do this morning. I'm going to buy a new one that makes time fly.

Finally, a woman appears from one of the offices, scanning the waiting room until her eyes stop on me. She's older than I am, probably in her late 30's, but very beautiful, with soft, black curls framing the warm, golden skin of her face. "Juliette?" she says, and I stand.

But instead of leading me to Master's office, she directs us to a sitting area with plush couches and cut crystal glasses set next to a carafe of water. She pours for both of us without spilling a drop. I want to ask where Master is, if he'll see me, if I've done something wrong, but I bite my lip. No need to start this off on the wrong foot.

"Has Antoine called?" I ask, instead. Probably best to find out what they know before I say anything. Maybe he's already asked me back, and I can just go and get this over with.

"No," she says. Her voice is gentle, like she's getting ready to let me down, and I launch automatically into defensive mode.

"So I'm just...waiting?"

She nods.

"Listen, I don't know what he said, but he took forever yesterday. *Forever.* I am committed to my lessons, but I don't have time to do that again. And also..." I pause and glance over at the woman, but her face doesn't give anything away. "If you want to know the truth, I thought he was too handsy with me."

"Didn't your last tutor touch you?"

What does she know about my tutors? What does she know about me? Enough, apparently. "Sure," I allow. "But Vlad was teaching me to dance—he had to touch me. That was all about moving the body, learning discipline and obedience. Antoine is just... a pervert." There. It feels good to just say what I mean for once, to let everything I've been thinking and feeling spill out of my mouth without a filter or a second thought. She's a woman. She'll understand.

She doesn't look horrified, though. Instead, she says, "Antoine painted me, you know. My husband commissioned a portrait for our first wedding anniversary."

Okay, I'm surprised. And confused. I thought it was bad enough that Antoine was putting his hands between my legs before my husband did, but while she was married? I would *never.*

"I loved his work on sight, but the process was hard," she admits. "I felt the way you did at first. Confused, and sometimes upset." She sips her water delicately before she says, "But then I realized that it wasn't about me and Antoine. It was about me and my husband. Antoine was just...our proxy. He only ever acted at my husband's behest, and with his consent. So when he touched me, it was like my husband was touching me. He never made a move that he and my husband hadn't choreographed and planned beforehand. It was all from him, and it was all for me." She shrugs. She's wearing a thin coral silk blouse, and the color is reflected in her cheeks, which glow with the memory. "After that, I could give myself over to him. And what we made together is profoundly gorgeous."

I consider this. It makes sense in theory, but it's still so different than anything I've ever thought about before. I know these men are training me for my husband, but it's different to try to imagine Antoine as an extension of him, allowed to do anything to my body that a husband might.

Well, not *everything*, surely?

"I think it would help if I knew what the rules were," I say. "Does the Agency know how far Antoine is allowed to go with me?"

She shakes her head. "It's no fun if you know what's coming," she says. "Preparation isn't the point. Just be there, and be patient, and you'll give your husband everything he wants."

She stands up to go, and I understand that this is all I'm getting from my visit here today; I won't get to see him or speak to Master directly. Again. It feels like a punishment, even if it isn't intended as one. Is this woman his proxy for him? Why won't he talk to me?

"Take care of yourself, Juliette," she says. "Master will call you when he needs to see you." She smiles and leaves, which means I have to go home and wait, praying that Antoine decides to take me back, and that I can get it right the second time around.

I'M asleep when I hear Master's voice, and for a moment, I think he's just a part of my dream. It wouldn't be unusual: in the last few weeks, I've woken up more than once with the phantom taste of him on my lips, the memory or palpable fantasy of his cock filling me up between my legs. But this time he's real, flesh and blood in the shadowy darkness, standing at the edge of my bed. Even at three o'clock in the morning, he's wearing a suit.

I sit up guiltily, trying to smooth my hair into place. "I'm sorry," I say, even though I'm not sure what I'm apologizing for.

"It's okay," he says. "I spoke to Antoine. He's agreed to take you on, and Juliette, you need to understand: the client has approved of his work."

I bow my head in a nod. I'm flooded with relief, but also adrenaline and anxiety. The woman at his office today said Antoine's process was difficult for the model, and if what I've seen already is any indication, she wasn't exaggerating. Will I be able to get through it? Now that I've been accepted, am I going to disappoint myself and, more importantly, Master again?

"Juliette," Master says, and I look up again, catching his gaze with mine.

My first impulse is to cast my eyes down, but I stop myself. I am Juliette Newmont, and I am ready for any challenge ahead of me.

"Yes, Master?"

"You will be in his studio at 8:32 tomorrow morning. You will do whatever he asks of you."

"I will," I repeat.

"These lessons are designed to teach you what the client wants you to learn," he says. "And they are not always what they appear. Don't try to figure them out. Just do as you're told, and you'll get what you need."

That's so much easier said than done. I wonder if Master has ever had to hold still against a desire that felt like it would burn him from the inside out, consume him and leave nothing but ash behind; I wonder if anyone's ever thrust his legs apart, made him shameless, looked at him like an object. I'm certain they haven't. He would never stand for it.

What does it mean, then, that I love it as much as I resent it? That the idea of sitting in front of Antoine tomorrow, on display, makes me almost as wet as looking at the shape of Master's shoulders silhouetted against my bedroom window?

"Lie down," Master says, and the words feel as physical as his hands on my body, stroking down my belly, making my spine go liquid. His voice feels like it's vibrating directly against my clit, a faint hum just where I need him. "Close your eyes. Count to ten. Out loud."

"One," I say, "two," my voice quavering slightly in the quiet of my room. I keep counting; when I get to ten, I pause, but he doesn't say anything. I hold still for a long time, waiting, but when I open my eyes, he's already gone.

3

I ARRIVE at the studio in the morning with a renewed determination. This is what my husband wants for me, and so I will do it; I'll let Antoine do whatever he wants with me, and know that his hands are an extension of my husband's. This will help me learn more about him, and be a better wife to him, when the time comes.

I'm even a little excited, actually. I felt guilty about my attraction to Antoine on our first day, disloyal for the way my body responded to him, but having him turn me on must be part of the point, and if that's what my husband wants, well, it will be no problem to give it to him.

I dress more simply for the second appointment; Master didn't give me any instructions about what to wear, and I know my clothes won't stay on long anyway. Still, Antoine circles me when I arrive, taking my hair out of its updo and mussing it with his fingers for a while, frowning at me before he speaks.

"Okay," he says. "We start with you sitting again. Legs spread. *Allez.*"

I settle onto the same white-draped surface from the first

time, my ass twinging slightly in protest; it's not exactly cushiony. The pain feels like a reminder too, though, of the last time Master visited me in the middle of the night, how he spanked me until I was so wet I was worried I'd soaked through my nightgown.

That memory combined with the way Antoine is looking at me, hungry and feral, sizzles through me like lightning. *All I have to do is sit here,* I remind myself. Antoine and my husband have decided on the rest of it. *You have to be an object,* Antoine said the first day. *No thoughts.*

Well, I am having thoughts, but they're all filthy, so maybe that doesn't count.

"Since you are so restless, I am thinking this will be a postcoital portrait," Antoine says. "And that way, we can put some of your energy to good use."

Before I have time to imagine what he might mean by that, he walks over and reaches between my legs, rubbing his fingers over my entrance where I'm slick and needy. I groan at the sensation, my hips pressing helplessly forward; I'm ready to come, imagining those long fingers inside me when he shushes me and unzips his pants to free his massive erection.

Antoine's cock is just as long and tall as he is; I'm close enough to smell the musk of his body mingling with the scent of my own, and just that combination makes me dizzy. I'm glad Master told me this had all been approved last night; it allows me to relax into my desire, to feel my mouth water and think of how ready I am to take my husband's cock.

Antoine takes the hand that's wet with my juices and strokes himself, a knowing grin spreading across his face as my wetness encircles him. He jerks himself off just as dispassionately as he sketched, fucking into his hand and forcing me to watch without offering myself in its place. I try not to imagine that same rhythm being applied to my body, that cock stuffed in my pussy; I feel myself clenching helplessly around nothing all the same.

Just before he comes, he tugs me in a little closer and aims so that cum ends up all over my breasts, dripping warm and wet on my nipples.

I reach between my legs to get myself a little relief. That has to be allowed. But he slaps my hand away with a *"Non, cherie.* Not today."

These rules suck.

He taps my bottom lip with one finger. "Open."

I do.

His cock is still in his hand. "Clean me up, *cherie,"* he commands.

Until this moment, sitting for Antoine has been a lot like ballet lessons with Vlad: he positions my body where he wants it, making me wetter every time. Vlad touched my aching, soaking pussy, but this is different. I've never touched a man's penis before, let alone taken it in my mouth. For a second, even though I was hungry for it a few minutes ago, I consider resisting; I had always thought I would save these experiences for my husband, that he would be my first in everything.

But Master said to obey Antoine the way I would obey him. He said I was being made into a toy, and it didn't matter who played with me before my husband did. He said this was what my husband wants, and I will give it to him.

Also, I want to. I have to admit that to myself: this is exactly what I want.

I lean forward and take Antoine's cock in my mouth. Even half hard he's still big enough to stretch my lips around; he tastes like bleach and skin and my mouth waters for more of the weight of a hard cock on my tongue, the scent of him in my nose; he keeps his hands in my hair as I lick him clean, lavishing him with all of the attention I've been holding myself back from giving. I can't believe I've never done this before, and I realize I've been moaning the whole time, suckling at him helplessly, trying to pull him deeper and deeper down.

When Antoine pulls me off, my mouth stays open for more, and he gives me his fingers for just a moment, letting me suck on them before he pulls them out and wipes them through the cum still covering my breasts.

"Soon," he says, wiping his hand—my spit and my juice and his cum, the mess of our bodies—across my face. "I will teach you to take a cock down your throat. But for now, I want the innocence. So. Turn towards the window," he says, tucking himself back into his pants.

He goes to wash his hands and I wait for him, pussy aching, nipples hard as pebbles, feeling wet and used and still needy all over. He's still barely touched me. When he comes back, he sits down and starts sketching again.

On my first day, the sketches were quick things, just studies, but this sitting stretches on for what feels like for-fucking-ever. The mess on my face dries and cracks; my butt hurts from sitting on this wooden pedestal for hours. The light is starting to go, but he doesn't stop sketching. He just adds a lamp, which takes so long to set up that I wonder if I'll survive this after all.

Since he's not working, I take the opportunity to try to chat him up. It gets boring just sitting there; I know he has to concentrate, but a little conversation wouldn't kill him, and it will make my afternoon much, much more pleasant. Maybe I'll even learn a bit about my husband along the way, since he and Antoine have apparently discussed me and what to do with me at some length. "So how did you get into painting porn?" I ask.

No response. When he goes to sit back in his chair and resume work, I try again. I should know not to provoke my teachers, but I've been sitting here for a long time, and I'm getting a little thirsty. He can't deny me something as basic as a drink, can he?

"Can I have water?" I ask.

More silence. I'm starting to feel a little dizzy. The problem with these tests is, they're difficult in a new way, every single time. And even though I've been warned and I've been told to just hold still and let Antoine do what he wants, I can't make myself do it. "Can't you take a picture? Paint from that?"

By the time the sun has slipped below the horizon I'm shameless. "I have to go to the bathroom," I say. He doesn't even look up from his sketch pad. "I should be home for dinner."

Finally, Antoine rumbles exactly four words, without even looking up from his work: "*Cherie*," he says. "Just go, then."

4

"I THINK I figured out what the problem was yesterday," is how Antoine greets me when I walk in the next morning.

Oh thank God. He's going to actually tell me what he wants, instead of letting me guess. Yesterday was hot, but if it wasn't going to get me closer to the finish line, it was useless.

"Strip," he says.

I pull my dress over my head. I chose not to wear lingerie today, hoping to get at least a little bit of a reaction out of Antoine, but he's unfazed by my naked body.

He takes in the weight of my breasts, the curve of my waist, with eyes like probing fingers, then and nods once. I'm already lightheaded with arousal, dizzy thinking about whether he'll let me taste his cock again today.

"Sit," he says.

The pedestal is set up again the same way it was yesterday: white sheets, white background. He's already done all of the lighting today, at least, so I won't have to hold my pose while he roots around for an extension cord or sets up another fill sheet.

"Show me your pussy," he says flatly.

Is he bored?

I'm ashamed of how wet I am, and I hesitate for just a moment.

He snaps his fingers, impatient with me, and the sound startles my legs apart. I'm spreading like I'm at the gynecologist, feet in stirrups. There's nothing he can't see.

He steps forward and kneels between my legs. It's not just my pussy that's visible to him, the plump curves of my ass, but the goosebumps that have risen on my skin, how my nipples are stiff already, begging for the touch of his fingers or tongue. My whole body strains towards his while he inspects me like an indifferent buyer in a car showroom.

"Come on," he says. "*Totalement.*" Then, with the flat of his hands, he spreads the lips of my pussy even further, so I'm completely and utterly exposed. I wonder if he can see my inner muscles pulsing helplessly, begging for something long and thick to clench around.

"Your turn," he says. "Make yourself useful, Juliette," and he takes my hand to replace his, spreading my lips wide.

He gets up and just stands there, looking at me, while I hold myself open for his gaze. He sees my most tender, sensitive parts. He sees how willing I am to do whatever he says. He sees how I react to being told what to do.

I try to imagine my husband in his place, seeing how responsive I am for him, how helplessly I want to be taken. But it's hard to picture a man I've never met, and the reality of Antoine keeps intruding. He doesn't look like a man who's experiencing desire, who's seeing his virginal bride's cunt pulse at the thought of his cock. All he's thinking about is his art, and he thinks about it for a long, long time.

I have to focus. I remember my father's words in the driveway the other morning: *he's going to pay top dollar for it.* *He*. My husband. My husband, not the fantasy of him but the reality, is on the other side of this endless process. I just have to go through Antoine to get to him.

Is there any way to make Antoine's inspiration come faster, I wonder? Some pose I could strike, something I could do that would mean we haven't wasted half the morning? All of yesterday's work has apparently been thrown out, and today, he hasn't even picked up a pencil yet.

Finally, he steps forward again. I don't move. He sticks a single finger in my pussy, as if he's testing a cake.

"Am I done?" I ask, trying to lighten the mood a little bit, to get him to *talk* to me.

Instead of answering, he sticks his wet finger in his mouth and sucks off my juices with an audible *pop*.

"Quite."

I wonder how I taste to him, if it's as intoxicating to him as his cock was to me yesterday.

"The problem was, yesterday, you weren't satisfied," Antoine says. "After you left, I realized you could tell in the pictures. So what I'm thinking is, I should fuck you, no? And then paint you when you're come-drunk and used, that pussy swollen from taking my cock all day. Lying with your legs spread for everyone to see just how badly you needed it."

My mind whirls. My body is begging me to say yes: to keep my legs spread just like this and let him slide himself in as deep as he will go. I imagine him pumping in and out of me, fucking me roughly until I scream; I imagine cleaning him up again with my mouth after, tasting both of us on his skin, and for a second I'm so worked up I can barely breathe.

But Antoine didn't command; he asked, which means I'm allowed to say no. And in my right mind, the part that's not just a crazed animal, it's not just that I've always expected to save my virginity for my husband—I want to. I want the first time someone takes me apart to happen with him. I'm happy to play with whoever he instructs me to play with, but if this is my decision, I'm going to refuse it. The woman at Master's office said every move Antoine made was choreographed with her husband, so it must mean something that he's giving me a choice.

"I'm saving myself for my husband," I say.

Antoine is unperturbed. "Fine, then," he says. "So go on and get yourself off. I will watch, then paint your satisfaction."

No command has ever been more welcome. My hands are already between my legs; all I have to do is hook two fingers inside of myself, where I'm already soaking wet and slippery soft. I rub my clit against the heel of my palm, the friction sparking along my spine and behind my eyes. I imagine my husband thinking of me, wherever he is.

With my free hand I reach up and pinch one of my nipples, and the interplay of sensations, my soft hand and that tiny lick of pain, pushes me over the edge even faster than I expected.

"Make it last, *cherie*," Antoine says, but too late. I come with a cry, shaking as the aftershocks tremble through my body.

When I look up, he's just getting himself settled at his easel.

Which means he didn't have time to sketch a thing.

My cheeks are bright red now, the embarrassment of my nudity and my eagerness and my easy orgasm all settling on me at once.

Antoine shakes his head just slightly. "Again," he says.

Again?

Oh God. This is the opposite of Master's endless delaying, dragging it out. And while it's at least a little bit welcome, I'm not even sure I can come again this quickly.

But I'm still wet, and as I start to stroke myself, I can feel the edge of another orgasm lurking somewhere in my body, ready to be coaxed out of me a little more carefully this time. I pull the fingers I'd tucked inside of myself out, gasping at the loss of fullness, and start to play with my nipples again, rolling them carefully between my finger and thumb. I keep my other palm pressed against my stomach, my fingers hovering just above my clit, their absence a tempting tease.

"Spread," Antoine commands, already bored, from his station at the sketch pad. "Keep your legs wide or I will tie them that way."

The idea cracks through me like a whip. I want to be good, but I want that, too. My pussy throbs. My thighs ache. Antoine draws a single line and then pauses, watching me.

I have the feeling it's going to be a long afternoon.

WHEN I GET HOME, I feel even worse than I did yesterday—I'm a mess of knotted muscles and aching soreness, everything from my cunt to my ass to my shoulders protesting having been made to hold the same position all afternoon—except when I was trying to make myself come for Antoine again and again and again.

Jane's waiting in my guesthouse. She helps me into the bath; then she massages my shoulders hard enough to hurt, because she's a living angel.

When I'm settled, she brings me dinner in my room, which is a blessing, since I don't think I could manage sitting up at the dinner table, then I launch into the story of the day.

"And after all of that," I say to Jane as she sips the last of her tea. "Three whole days in the studio, he isn't even sure it's the right picture! At this rate, I'm worried I'll see another birthday before I can plan a wedding. I can't take it much longer."

She sighs in sympathy. "I guess you have to go back again tomorrow?"

"Yeah. He offered me the day off if I wanted, but I didn't take it."

"Why not?"

"Because a day off means another day when I have to wait. I'm no closer to meeting my husband. No closer to finding out who's behind all of this. It sucks, so I want to get it over with as fast as possible. "

"That makes sense."

I've mostly finished my food, and Jane stands to clear my plates away, ringing a discreet bell that will let someone in the kitchens know to come collect them. Some nights she cooks for us, some nights I skip dinner, but tonight she read my mind and had Eloise make us dinner.

"I wonder," she says. "You said all of his pictures were super sexual, right? Maybe he doesn't want you to be demure. Maybe you should try being hotter—just like, full-on sexy—for him. Maybe that would help?"

I nod slowly. That would make sense. The women in Antoine's other pictures weren't just posing; they looked like they were about to be fucked, or just had been, like if you could walk inside the frame you could fuck them, too. But how can I convey that when I won't fuck Antoine, or anyone else besides the man who's bought me in marriage?

"I have some arnica that might help with those aches," Jane offers. "Come sit in the living room and I'll set up the diffuser with some lavender." She gives me a hand as I stand up. It feels good to get some blood flowing to my muscles, even as they protest on our short walk from one room to another.

I settle myself on the little velvet couch while she finds what she's looking for. There's a bouquet on the table, a spray of white flowers that smell so sweet and delicate I make myself get up again just to press my face into their petals. How did I miss this when I came in earlier? Was I that exhausted?

"Jane!" I call. "Where are these from?"

"Bruce," she says shyly, returning with a small white tube in one hand. "For me, but I didn't want to be the only one to enjoy them, so I brought them here. Is that okay?"

"Of course!"

Bruce and Jane's romance has been going on about as long as I've been under Master's tutelage. Our caretaker's gorgeous, but rough around the edges. He caught Jane snooping outside my window one night and gave her a life-changing spanking. I haven't heard about him for a while, though, so I thought things might have cooled off between them. Apparently not.

"I think he likes me."

"You *think*?" All thoughts of my own body are forgotten for the moment. "Are you guys serious? How far have you gone?"

Jane fingers a velvet petal for a moment before replying. "Well," she says carefully. "Not very. He's kind of old-fashioned."

Part of me is relieved my friend hasn't jumped ahead of me.

"Well, we both have to wait then!" I chirp.

She smiles—but not fast enough for me to miss the sullen frown that preceded it.

Jane was thirteen when her father—her only living parent and our butler—died. Daddy kept her with me, putting money in her trust. When I turned seventeen, we both moved from the main house to our own guesthouses on the compound. The money went into her pocket and I became her job. She's had the same tutors, the same trips, the same life, the same lessons...except for these latest ones.

So, though it's strange to think of her having done something I haven't experienced yet, her frown tells me something else is going on.

"Jane," I say. "What's—?"

"It's nothing." She points to the bouquet. "Should I put an aspirin in the water?"

"Is there something else with Bruce you're not telling me? Is he hurting you? Saying bad things?"

"Nope." She goes to the kitchen, presumably for aspirin, and I follow her, glad to give her problems some attention.

"Are you sure?" I was right. She grabs a bottle of aspirin from my cabinet and pops it open with the same painted-on smile. "Please don't lie to save my feelings."

That gets a crestfallen sigh out of her.

"It's nothing," she says, admitting it's *something* while tumbling a little white pill into her palm. I cross my arms and lean on the door jamb, ready to listen, and she snaps the top back on the bottle. "Okay, since you're not going to let it be…"

"I am not."

"Don't take this personally." It's not a command, but a plea. "It's just, I've always had to wait for you. To move out of the big house. To get a driver's license. Even to do my own shopping. It's my job, so it's okay. But now, I'm waiting for you to get married so I can start my own life and it's just one thing after another." She holds back tears. "I know it's not your fault. I'm sorry."

"Don't worry!" I rush to hug her. "Don't be sorry!"

I hate to think of both of us being this impatient to start our lives, but adding sexual frustration into the mix for her just isn't right. I have Master's and my husband's inscrutable tastes to deal with, but if she wants Bruce, I want to help her move ahead. I run through what I know about seduction, which isn't much, but I've picked up a few things along the way.

"I can't change the wait, and I'm sorry about that, but for the other thing…I have a plan." I sound more confident than I am. "Let's move this thing with Bruce along."

"I've tried everything."

"I'm still learning how to do what Master wants, and what my husband wants, but you? Trust me, you haven't tried *everything*."

5

I'VE ALREADY BEEN to the Agent Provocateur boutique twice this month picking up things for Master, so I direct the driver to take Jane and me to another store, a secret little boutique that stocks only limited-edition pieces from small designers. I've spent many afternoons walking up and down the narrow aisles, dreaming of wearing the bustiers gleaming with crystals sewn on by Italian nuns or panties made of lace hand-stitched in French ateliers. I've never had to adorn my body for my husband, so I never had a reason to buy anything, but Jane is in pursuit of a man she wants, and for me…well, things are changing, too. Wearing lingerie for my husband has taken on new meaning.

Jane steps through the bright red door and sucks in a breath. "Oh my God," she murmurs. "Juliette. This is…"

"Isn't it?" I sweep my hand to encompass everything in the room, the delicate pink satin garter set that reminds me of my ballet outfits, and a leather bodysuit paired with a whip that comes with a crystal-encrusted hilt. "Pick out whatever you want. My treat, of course."

"Are you sure?"

"I'm so sure. At least one of us should be getting some, and Bruce is only human. If he sees you in one of these, I know you'll get what you want."

The shop's proprietress is an old lady named Teresa. She looks like a fairy-tale witch who's gotten a makeover, and what I find out is that she has a sorcerer's knack for knowing what you want better than you do.

"Juliette!" she calls. "What brings you in today?"

"We're actually shopping for my friend Jane," I tell her. "She needs something that will make a man unable to say no to her."

Teresa looks Jane up and down approvingly. "That shouldn't be too hard," she says. "Come with me, darling. I think I have just the thing."

While they shop, I wander the aisles by myself. The store is full of treasures Teresa knows better than anyone, but there's also something magical about losing myself in the maze of tulle and silk, leather and lace.

All of it is luxuriant and beautiful, but none of it quite speaks to me today. I consider a bra and panty set made of midnight-blue silk and crusted in sapphires; I stroke the shimmering silk of a cerulean negligée.

"Juliette!" Jane calls.

I go to the back of the store and find Jane standing on a pedestal, surrounded by softly lit mirrors, with Teresa admiring her handiwork. She's put Jane in something simple: a matched set made of intricate ivory lace. A bright green stone that matches her eyes glistens between her breasts, and the balconet of the bra is cut so low that it almost looks like she'll spill right out of it. Jane looks like a gemstone, lit up and glowing from within.

"It's too much," she says. "Right?"

"Jane."

"Bruce is—"

"Bruce," I remind her, "has never seen anything like it."

Jane regards her reflection. "Well," she admits. "That's probably true."

"Do you like it?"

"I love it. I had no idea I could look so..." She drifts off, unable to find words.

"Sexy," Teresa says. "A man could eat you up in this. He will not be able to resist. No way."

"See?" I say. "We'll take it."

Teresa turns to me. "Nothing for you today?"

I shake my head. "I think I might have problems even lingerie can't solve."

She laughs at me. "I doubt that, Ms. Newmont."

I follow her to the front of the store, lost in the cloud of my thoughts. While she's wrapping up Jane's purchase, though, I spot something I missed before. It's a gold silk suspender set, paired with matching bra, panties, and garters. The material is the same color as my hair in the sunlight, and I imagine a man's hands slipping under my skirt to feel its softness, undressing me to find me shimmering in front of him.

I realize too late that the man I'm picturing isn't anonymous, and it's definitely not my husband. It's Master's vivid green eyes going bright at the sight of me, Master's big, strong hands tugging the fabric over my hip bone, caressing me between my legs where I've soaked that expensive silk straight through.

I have to stop doing this. Master isn't the man who bought me, and I know it perfectly well. Still, though, the lingerie will look good on me no matter who it's for, and what's the point of having all of this money if I don't spend it? I may feel awful right now, wrung out and exhausted, but when I finally wear this, I'll be radiant with triumph.

By now, Teresa has caught me looking. "Yes," she says

approvingly. "And if you like that, I have another one we should try on you, too."

———

In the car home, Jane is quiet—too quiet. Usually with me she's a chatterbox; we talk about everything and nothing, filling our hours together with conversation. I wait until we're back in the guesthouse to ask her about it, though. The partition is up in the car, but I know people gossip, and I don't want Rowan overhearing anything that could link Jane to Bruce before she's ready.

"Jane," I ask as we walk back into the house. "Is everything okay?"

She smiles. "I'm fine."

"You just seem..." I shrug. "A little off. Don't you like your present?"

"I do!" she says. "Of course I do. You're so generous. I just... I wonder if it will be enough, is all."

"You heard Teresa. It will be more than enough."

Jane is looking at the floor when she says, "What if *I'm* not enough, then?"

"Jane!" I drop my bags on the floor and wrap her up in a hug. I hate that she feels this way. Jane is so beautiful, and such a wonderful friend. Bruce would be lucky to have her. Why can't he just say so? What is wrong with him?

When I pull away again, Jane's eyes are glassed with unshed tears. "I don't want you to think I'm jealous of you," she says. "Because I'm *not*. Or I don't want to be. You deserve everything you've been given, and you've worked so hard in your training. I just wish sometimes... I wish that I could be trained, too. I feel like I'm making it up as I go along, and maybe that's why I'm failing."

"You are not failing."

"Oh, Juliette. You always believe in me." She twists her mouth into an unhappy expression. "But if he doesn't want me..."

I sink down onto the couch, and Jane follows suit. "First of all, he sent you flowers," I remind her. "Why would he do that if he didn't want you? Bruce has never sent me flowers. In fact, no one has ever sent me flowers. And look at me," I add. "I'm getting trained, but I'm just as frustrated as you are."

"That can't be true." Jane shakes her head. "You took me to the store tonight. You had a plan. I just... When I think of all that you're learning, I can't help but want it for myself. You're being prepared to do exactly what you need to do. I think I could be good for him if I just knew *how*."

I let out a laugh. "They *don't* tell me exactly what to do," I say. "That's the point! Or they say, strip and sit over there, but they don't say how long I'm meant to sit for. They put me in a ballet studio but never explain that I'm supposed to be studying obedience, so I spent weeks thinking my future husband really cares whether or not my pirouettes are perfect, when in fact, he just wants me to learn how to do what I'm told." I haven't even told Jane about what the woman in Master's office said yet: how she said that Antoine is a proxy for my husband. How I'm supposed to let him touch me the way I would let my husband touch me. And how badly I want that, even though I still feel like I'm not supposed to.

My voice drops, and I'm aware that I'm about to say something that feels like a confession, something I've barely admitted to myself so far. "I know I'm lucky," I say. "But honestly, training has been confusing for me. Most days I have no idea if I'm good at it or not. And on the worst days... I'm not even sure it's good for me."

Jane shuffles over and leans her head on my shoulder. "I

didn't know," she says. "I guess I just thought... I thought it might make everything simpler. And I would like for things to be simple, Juliette."

I nod, and I know she can feel the motion from where her head is resting. "Me too," I agree. "Me too."

I ARRIVE at Antoine's the next morning wearing one of my purchases from Teresa: a black playsuit made mostly of silk straps. There are suspenders that attach to lace garters on my thighs; the straps cross my chest like a harness, displaying my breasts without covering them up. "You can wear this with a bra and panties," Teresa informed me, but I like it better without: the sight of my bare cunt and hard nipples, every vulnerable part of me framed by these long black lines, echoes of restraints he could use to hold me in place if he needed to. I shiver lightly at the thought.

If this isn't inspiring, I don't know what will be.

Antoine seems to be into it, too. "Good," he says when I strip for him. "This is very good. You can leave this on for now. I have a new inspiration for a pose."

I thought a lot about what Jane said to me yesterday about needing to be sexier. Maybe this is how I can get this all over and done with before I lose my mind. Antoine won't tell me what he wants, and maybe figuring it out is the test.

Instead of climbing onto the pedestal, I kneel down where the white canvas puddles on the floor and get on my hands and knees, opening my mouth for him. The more vulgar the better, I think—that certainly seems to be what Antoine likes.

At first, I'm nervous about taking even this much control, but his eyes light up at the sight of me. He strokes himself in his pants as he takes in the sight: how eager I am, posed for his pencils as much as for his cock.

Then he unzips and pulls himself out. I'm already wet, pussy pulsing at the way I've exposed myself, but my mouth waters, too, at the sight of him. At first I think it'll be like it was the first day; he'll get himself off and only let me clean up.

Then he walks over to me, and my heart starts pounding in my chest. My senses are overwhelmed by the nearness of this powerful man who hasn't said a word and still has me mostly naked on his floor, quivering with need.

Your husband wants this, I remind myself, and that just makes it hotter: one man in front of me, about to use my body, and behind him, the phantom sense of my husband, invisible and unknown, but still controlling my every move, directing my pleasure and Antoine's as well as his own.

"You have sucked a cock before, or no?" he asks.

"No."

"*Bon.* I will instruct you. Open your mouth and say *ahh* like you are at the doctor."

"Ahh."

"That is the sound of your throat opening, and it's the sound you'll make when I fuck it. Understand?"

"Yes."

"Open."

Antoine feeds himself slowly into my mouth, savoring the slide of his skin on my tongue, nudging at the back of my throat. As overwhelming as he was yesterday, it's even more when he's hard, and I'm gasping a little at the size and weight of him.

"Resist gagging," he demands. "Just put your hands behind your back and take it."

He presses deeper and deeper inside on every thrust. He

doesn't touch me anywhere else, and my body feels electric with want, like lightning searching for ground.

Then he stops, pulls my hair to make sure he has my attention. "Now, we change," he says. "You don't just take it. Suck me, Juliette. Show me what you can do."

I pull back a little, nuzzling at the head of his dick, feeling him leaking on my tongue already. "Slow," he says. "Yeah, like that." I take him as deep as I can and then pull back again, bobbing my head in a rhythm, letting him set the pace. "Sit up a little bit," he adds. "Let me see those gorgeous tits. Are your nipples hard for me? Are you as wet as you were yesterday? I could slide right in there, you know. Your pussy wants me. You can't hide it, Juliette."

My mouth is too full of cock to answer, so I just moan in response.

"Good girl," he says. "Faster, now. Suck my cock like a little whore."

My body obeys instantly, and I know that all of the hours spent under Vlad's tutelage weren't for nothing. As soon as Antoine tells me what he wants, I give it to him, whether it's to fuck my throat or to have me nuzzle the head of his cock, lapping at it like a kitten.

It's intoxicating, having all of his attention on me like this, his dick in my mouth, my body being used for his pleasure. But also, a small part of my attention is always on the clock. My jaw is starting to get sore, and my knees ache from the wooden floors underneath the canvas. The next time he pulls back, I reach up a hand to wrap around him, hoping I can use both to make him come a little bit faster.

He smacks it away immediately.

"Don't be lazy," he says. "Mouth only."

So much for that idea. After that he seems to slow down on purpose again, instructing me to close my mouth so he can rub his cock against my lips and on my cheeks. As usual,

I have no control in the situation, so I try to give him everything I have, praying I won't be on my knees like this all day. When will he start sketching?

"Now open wide. All the way so I can fuck your mouth." He thrusts down, fucking my throat until he pulls out abruptly in order to come all over my face. Even though he hasn't ordered me to, I hold perfectly still, and it's even dirtier than the first time he came on me—there's something so debased about him just painting my face with his cock, spurting on me like I'm not even his muse, little more than a canvas. My cunt is so wet I can feel it dripping down my bare legs, but he just steps back and looks at me.

"Perfect," he breathes.

Victory.

He can see how worked up I am. He cups the back of my head, fingers trailing down my neck; I feel every touch of his skin on mine like the first spark of a raging bonfire. "You did a good job," he says. "Was that your first?"

I nod.

"You want me to fuck you now?"

I want his cock in me so badly I could scream. But also, I made a decision, and I'm going to stick to it. That's a form of obedience, too.

"Still saving it for my husband," I tell him.

Antoine releases me with a sigh. "If you say so," he says, picking up a sketch pad. "Sit up, and lace your fingers behind your head. Show off how I put my cum all over your face."

As interesting as the first hour of the session was, it's crystal clear that it's going to be a long day.

6

ANTOINE and I fall into a routine. It's almost like my mornings at the ballet studio, letting Vlad position my body over and over again, except filthier. Every day I show up and take off my clothes and touch myself in front of Antoine's impassive gaze, rubbing my clit and fucking my fingers, moaning shamelessly as I work myself towards orgasm. Once I'm done, he pulls out his cock and lets me suck him off; I've gotten better and better at taking him down my throat. I let him use my mouth and make a mess of my face when he comes. I think of my husband while he fucks my face and the idea of him lights me on fire every time.

The taste of him still makes me wet, and there's not a day that goes by that I don't consider letting him fuck me. But I don't.

He changes my position to all fours, mouth open, face covered in cum, and starts all over. All the muscles I spent weeks defining and developing at the barre now exist solely to hold me in place for as long as Antoine paints, and somehow, I'm just as sore at the end of the day as I was when I was dancing for eight hours instead of just kneeling, mouth open, my tutor's cum drying on my face.

But even when Antoine offers me a day off, I don't take it. I have to get this thing over with. My husband is on the other side of that canvas the painter won't let me see.

Sometimes I try to get Antoine to talk about his clients in the hopes that he'll accidentally give me a peek at what my husband is like, since asking directly has never gotten me anywhere. "Who buys this stuff?" I ask one afternoon. We've broken for lunch, and we're sitting at a small table near the window, Antoine in his painting clothes, me still with my pussy and tits on display, sitting bare-assed on a wooden barstool. I imagine Juliette from three months ago seeing me, and how horrified she would be. Horrified and turned on, too, even if she wouldn't want to admit it. "Is it horny old guys who can't get any, or is it more commissions from lovers, like this one?"

"My clients come from all over," Antoine replies. "Each has his own motivations, his own desires."

Well that's incredibly useless. "What about a piece like mine?" I ask, trying to redirect us to somewhere more specific. "Who do you think might be interested?"

"I used to have a client who had me paint every girl he fucked," Antoine says, all but ignoring my question. Or is he? Is this client my husband? I sort of hope not. "Every one of them," Antoine continues. "He was lucky he had such good taste—they were all beauties, and I didn't mind. But it made it hard to focus on anything else, and I believe my artistic practice suffered as a result. I was glad when he got married, and I could focus on other things for a while."

Okay, so not my husband. I'm relieved. I know he doesn't mind if I'm with other men before him, so I assume he's been with other women, and that's fine, but I don't want a hall of their portraits in our house together.

"Do you have any favorite clients?" I try, and as soon as I've said it, I realize it was a bad idea.

"You are chatty today," he says. "Come, let me use your mouth for something else." He has me kneel between his legs right where we are, and suck him off while he finishes his sandwich; when I'm done, I have cum in my eyelashes and crumbs in my hair. After that, I stop asking questions and concentrate harder than ever on giving him what he wants so I can get through it as fast as possible.

Then, finally, Antoine declares himself done, and still, he won't let me see myself as he sees me.

WHEN THE DAY of the unveiling finally comes, I'm ecstatic. I wake up extra early to do my hair and makeup; I slip on the gold lingerie set I got at Teresa's—a secret personal trophy that I can hold close under my dress. I'm too buzzy to be alone, so I bring my breakfast into Jane's house so I can tell her it's the big day. I didn't see her when I came in last night, so I haven't had the chance to tell her the good news yet.

"Today is the day!" I announce, bouncing over the threshold as soon as she's opened the door. Jane is still wearing her pajamas, and she looks like she just got out of bed. I put the tray on her kitchen table and offer her a piece of my toast as an apology for waking her up. "Coffee?"

"Yes, please." She takes the toast. "The day for what?"

I hand her a mug just the way she likes it. Light and sweet, just like her.

"This part of my training is done! That's why I was at the studio so late last night—Antoine was finishing things up, and he wanted to get every detail perfect. Today he unveils it to Master, and then..." I haven't told Jane yet what I suspect about the painting's buyer, so I swallow the end of my sentence. "And then I move on to the next part of my journey," I say.

"Congratulations. You deserve it. You've worked so hard."

"And what about you? No news?"

Jane shakes her head. "No news."

I heave a frustrated sigh on her behalf. She's worn the lingerie she bought at Teresa's every day for weeks now, carefully hand-washing it and hanging it to dry overnight every night. But every time she shows up at the maintenance shed where Bruce works, he sends her away—sometimes immediately, sometimes after making her wait for ten or fifteen minutes, but always eventually he says, "I'm too busy right now. Come back later." Several times he's instructed her to come back at a specific time—not Master specific, but things like, "at three, when I'm done with the lawns" or "tomorrow morning, first thing." Except when Jane shows up, he's not there.

"When I went yesterday, there was a note," Jane says, a mix of sadness and hope in her voice.

"What did it say?"

"That if I couldn't wait around for him anymore, he'd understand."

"But you still want to, right?"

"I do. It's driving me crazy, but the waiting also makes it hotter. Like when he finally does touch me, after all of this—I might explode."

Then what choice does she have? At least she doesn't have to sit still covered in bodily fluids while she waits. "So keep waiting," I say. "He'll come around. He has to."

I check my watch and realize I have to go if I want to be at the studio on time. I cram one last bite of toast into my mouth and kiss Jane on the cheek. "It's all going to work out," I tell her. "Just be patient. You'll see."

7

I AM PERFECTLY ON TIME, but Master is already in the studio when I arrive. As always, I'm undone by his presence: the cold command in his eyes, the curl of his mouth and the sharpness of his body's raw power contained in a perfectly tailored suit. For a moment I imagine Antoine asking me for one last performance: putting me on my knees and making me suck both of their cocks, their cum painting me like a canvas. My nipples stiffen beneath my dress, and I know they can both see it, but that doesn't even make me feel ashamed anymore.

What I feel instead is a rush of disappointment: as happy as I am to see Master, he's the only other person in the studio, which means this isn't how I meet my husband.

Him not being here for the unveiling doesn't necessarily mean anything. Once I figure out who the buyer is, I'll at least have a name, and that will be something to hold on to.

The canvas sits on an easel, which is covered in a white sheet, and even though it's quite large—at least four feet tall —it feels oddly small to me. Weeks of my life on my knees, swallowing Antoine's cock, wringing orgasms out of myself until my muscles cramped and I could barely stand, and that's it. Just one painting. It had better be a good one.

"Juliette," Master says as he holds his hand out to the covered easel. "Please show me what you've done."

That's when I notice Antoine's face. He's not exactly beaming with pride and excitement.

I pull off the sheet and am confronted by an image I recognize, and also don't. That's me on my knees, mouth open, tits framed by the black lines of my playsuit, jizz drying in the hollow of my throat. In some sense, I am clearly trying to please; the pose is super-porny, and Antoine has rendered the details of my body with his signature precision and detail. If you don't look at it too closely, the picture is hot, something you could jerk off to like a *Playboy* centerfold.

But was that the expression on my face the whole time? The woman in the picture is doing a sexy pose, her body communicating availability, but her gaze is fixed on the door, like she wants to get out of there as soon as possible. For all of Antoine's skill, it's still an ugly picture. And that's clearly the model's fault.

My fault.

There's a very long silence.

"Well," Master says finally. "That's not what my client was hoping for, now is it?"

The words hit me like a brick to the sternum. In that long silence, I'd almost hoped he would see something different in it, or allow me to get away with it, but of course he won't. He shouldn't.

Antoine sighs. "This is what she gave me."

Master won't even look at me, and my cheeks heat with fury and shame. I had thought I had this whole process figured out, that after my difficulties with Vlad, everything would be smooth sailing from here on out. I did do everything Antoine asked me to do. And I got off on it. But it was a means to an end. You can see that impatience, that distance and lack of focus, in every one of Antoine's brushstrokes.

So here I am again, disappointing Master, disappointing my tutor. Wasting everyone's time, including my own. I wouldn't want my husband to see me like this. I wouldn't marry the woman in this painting, and I can't imagine he would want to, either.

"Antoine," Master says. "What are we going to do? Try again?"

God, please no. I want to get this right but the thought of reliving all those boring hours is enough to make me glad when Antoine shakes his head.

"I don't paint the same girl twice."

Antoine must have known the painting would come out this way—why didn't he warn me? Ask me to change my expression, or better yet, paint me in some other moment? I would have done anything he asked of me. Wasn't that the point?

"Antoine told me what to do," I hear myself say. "It's as much his fault as it is mine."

"Juliette." Master's tone is firm and commanding, and even through my panic, it goes straight to my clit.

"Master," I reply. "Isn't the painter's job to help his subject pose? You have no idea how long I knelt for him—what he made me do, how long I waited. If he wanted me to look different—"

"Juliette," Master snaps, and this time, my mouth shuts automatically.

"Do you remember the first time you touched yourself for me?" Antoine asks, into my silence. "You made yourself come before I could even sit down at my easel to sketch. You were eager and impatient from the moment you walked through my doors, always asking for something—water, a snack, to go home for dinner. And your desire... You were hungry for cock, but your mind was always elsewhere. No pose could have changed that. You didn't want to be here, and it was visible in every movement you made, every shadow that crossed your face. There was nothing I could do about it. The man who owns you commissioned a painting, so I painted what I saw. If you do not like what you see..." He trails off, shrugs, like he has no interest in what happens to me next.

"She is right," he says. "She did what I asked. She let me use her mouth however I wanted. That's what you see in front of you. That's all she was able to give."

My heart crumples in my chest. All those weeks of kneeling, throat raw from taking him deep and then deeper, making myself come for him again and again—and I have nothing to show for it. An ugly painting, another disappointed tutor, and a wedding that's further away than ever.

"And only the mouth," Antoine says, still mostly addressing Master. I feel like a schoolgirl who's been naughty, except there's no delicious spanking coming for me next. "She says she is saving herself for her husband, like that cunt is a precious flower that will wilt if someone else touches it. *Non.* If she was open—if she was ready—maybe things would have been different. But this is no good, and I've wasted enough of my time on this little American prude."

Master turns to me. There's no hiding the fact that I have tears in my eyes.

"Juliette," he says. "Do you *want* to do this training?"

Daddy asked me the same question in the driveway a few weeks ago, and I rejected it out of hand; of course I want to get married. That's what I've always wanted. What I've prepared my whole life for. It's the reason I've acquired my skills—my languages and my understanding of diplomacy, as well as my taste and style. I know as much about advanced mathematics as I do about art history. I can charm world leaders and Hollywood power brokers. I don't know much about grocery shopping, but I've learned to make scrambled eggs from Michelin-starred chefs.

But what if I didn't want it?

That's never been discussed, and it doesn't matter. I will do as I'm told. I'll finish what I started, and maintain my track record as a perfect student. I will please my father and marry well, and *then*—once I've secured my position—figure out the rest of my life.

Just as I'm thinking this, Master speaks. "It's taking you too long to consider this," he says. "And that tells me everything I need to know."

Tears spring to my eyes as forcefully as if I'd been slapped. Helpless, I drop to my knees in front of him, my bare skin protesting another interlude with the wood floors, which are now sticky with still-wet paint. All of this morning's pleasant thoughts about my lingerie and my success are forgotten. I'll do anything if Master just lets me stay.

I don't want to leave him.

I don't want to lose him.

"Please," I hear myself saying, my voice distant in my own ears. "Please don't do that. I'll start over. I was just thinking. I don't want it to be over. I don't, I swear."

Master's expression doesn't change; it seems he's looking through me more than at me, like I'm barely even in the room for him anymore. "Not everyone's cut out for the life you were born into," he says, and his compassion is worse than his fury. It feels like pity. It makes my skin crawl. "There's no shame in it. So what we're going to do with you is—"

I don't want to hear whatever he's about to say next. "I want it," I say, my words cutting his sentence neatly in half. "I can make it. I swear I have what it takes."

Master doesn't say anything, just walks over until he's standing directly in front of me, his crotch with its sizable bulge just inches away from my face. The scent of him this close is overwhelming—his own soft musk mixed with the faint lemon in his cologne. I want to bury my face in his thigh. Does he want me to suck him off? My mouth is already watering at the thought. Should I turn around and let him spank me? Am I supposed to guess, or to wait?

I'm paralyzed by my own racing mind. Finally, he offers me a hand, and I take it. He urges me to stand, and I obey.

I try to brush myself off, but my skirt is wrinkled and there's paint on my knees. Somewhere in the background, Antoine is saying something—he sounds excited—but I can't make myself focus on his words. My world has narrowed down to Master's face, his hand in mine. Is this the last time he'll touch me? The weight of my failure feels crushingly enormous, like I've lost everything in the world that ever mattered to me.

"I'll take care of it," Master says, and for one more second I let myself believe that this isn't over, that there's something I can do to save myself. "I'll call your father," he continues, and my world goes as dark as my future.

8

I COLLAPSE onto the couch to sob, and sob, and sob.

I can't stop seeing the painting in my mind, and the longer I think about it, the more clearly I can see myself: scheming the whole time to make everything hurry up, go faster, go exactly the way I wanted it to. Outwardly following commands, but on the inside, I was always concentrating on myself and my wants and needs. I never thought through what Antoine wanted from me, or why my husband needed me there.

Most of all though, the thing that stings and pricks and cuts me with its teeth is the look on Master's face as he walked me out. He isn't one for big displays of emotion; I wept, but he just looked resigned. Like he hadn't wanted it to come to this, but wasn't surprised that it had, either.

"You're home early." Jane peeks in the door during a pause in my hysterics.

"Because I'm a failure." I start sobbing all over again.

Jane does her best to comfort me. She makes me tea and brings me a plate of cookies with raspberry jam in the middle. She coaxes me out of my tight dress and silly lingerie and into some soft leggings and an oversized cashmere sweater that feels like a cloud settling around me. She doesn't ask me anything. She lets me mourn the time I wasted while Antoine was working. If only I could have relaxed a little bit. If only I could have just...been there, instead of being so focused on the future that all I did was ruin it.

The sun is sliding west in the sky when Jane replaces my half-drunk tea and plate of cookie crumbs with a bowl of chicken soup.

"I'm not hungry," I tell her.

"You don't have to eat," she assures me. But her instincts are correct. If I keep crying I might permanently dehydrate myself, so I aim for distraction.

"Can you tell me about your day?"

"I went to see him while you were out," she says. "Bruce. I thought, if today is the day for Juliette, then today is the day for me, too. So instead of just...hanging out, I bent myself over the toolshed with my skirt hiked up. I wanted him to know exactly what I was offering. I wanted to give it to him, if he'd take it."

In spite of myself, I feel a heat rise in my body. I remember exactly how I felt that first day, bent over Master's desk, my panties in a silver tray in front of me. I hadn't even met him yet, and already I was wet with a daydream of a stranger's eyes looking between my legs. I was so young a few weeks ago.

"It took two hours," Jane says. "Two hours of waiting. My knees hurt. My ribs hurt. My butt got cold. I thought about your bruises. I thought about leaving."

I'm so wrapped up in the story that I don't realize I've reached for the soup and taken a spoonful until the liquid is sliding down my throat. It's one of our cook's specialties, and I remember why every time I taste it: the broth is rich with garlic and fragrant with lemon, comforting without being overwhelming. I take another bite.

"But then he showed up."

"And?" I'm happy for Jane—I am—but part of me feels even more worthless, knowing how patient she was, thinking she got what she wanted. "What did he say?"

"Not a word."

"Oh no, that's terrible."

A sly smile creeps across her face.

"He kicked my legs apart," she says, and my body pulses to hear more. "Pushed my panties aside, and picked up a screwdriver from the tool bench. I didn't know what to think. Then he slid the handle inside of me, slowly at first. Then faster."

I can imagine it all too well: the cool, unyielding plastic where she wanted hot, throbbing flesh. The feeling of pressure and fullness but not enough. God, why are men so maddening?

"He fucked me with it for a while," she says. "But he wouldn't let me come. Every time I started getting close he would stop and pull it out. I've never been so exposed in my life. He could see everything: how badly I wanted him. How I'd let him do anything."

My bowl of soup is finished, but it doesn't account for the fire in my belly.

"Finally," she says, "I was starting to get really close— closer than he'd let me get so far—I was shaking all over, feeling these waves everywhere in my body. And then he just stopped."

"He stopped?"

"Walked away to start the lawnmower, and left me with the screwdriver sticking out of me. Enough to drive me crazy, but not enough to make me come. But it was also...

anyone could have come in and seen what I'd let him do to me."

"What did you do after that?"

Jane shrugs. "What could I do? I didn't want to leave. So I waited more. Practiced my kegels."

Jane and I are both being tormented within an inch of our lives. I have no idea how she endured that. Maybe being in the program is no different than being outside of it. And if so, maybe my being outside of it is for the best, after all.

It's a bitter pill to swallow; though it is jagged and uncomfortable to sit with. What is my future if it doesn't look like the one that's been planned for me since forever?

Jane goes to clear my bowl, and I pick up my phone and dial my father's number. I haven't heard from him all day; I had sort of been expecting to be summoned to dinner, the same way I was when I almost got kicked out on my first day.

The phone rings and rings, and eventually it goes to voicemail. I don't leave a message; I don't know what to say, even to my own father. I'm sure either him or the Master will be in touch with bad news soon enough.

I DREAM I'm in a room full of men in tuxedos. I'm naked, but not ashamed. I'm panicked that they're all ignoring me. I feel Master in the room, but I can't find him. Then I smell his cologne. Then I hear his breathing.

His voice is the last confirmation that he's come into my room in the middle of the night, again.

"Get up." The dream's over. I wake up. He's just a shadow against the moonlit window, leaning down to snap off my covers.

"What?" I'm still disoriented and now I'm cold. The bathroom light goes on. I squint, and when my eyes adjust, he's not a shadow in the bathroom doorway, but a half-lit man in a full suit.

"I said get up," he reminds me. "And I don't want to say it again."

I'm out of bed like a shot, nightgown falling over my knees. He points to a spot in the center of the bathroom, and I stand there, placing my feet so there are three six-inch tiles between them. My nipples are dark and hard under the thin satin.

"Take off your clothes," he says. "Everything."

As I do it, he sits on the same plush chair as the last time he was in here with me. He crosses an ankle over the knee I rubbed against and watches me strip. I fold my nightgown and underwear, place them on the counter and resume my position for his inspection.

"You've never failed at anything in your life," he says. "This is turning into a problem."

I want to ask what kind of problem, but the shock of hearing the word *failure* in reference to my life is too shocking to answer.

"Failure is not something you can beg your way out of. It's not something you can try to avoid next time if there is no next time. I don't want to make you too nervous to perform, but the consequences are pretty dire, Juliette. For you. For your family."

"How?" I interrupt him, then realize my error. "Sorry."

"It's not for me to say how. Suffice it to say, your family, your heritage, it's very rare, and you've been living its privileges. There are penalties for not keeping your end of the deal."

"I want to, Master!" I'm not going to cry, but damn, I feel a good bawl creep up my throat.

"I know." From his pocket, he takes a black velvet box the

size of wristwatch packaging and stands in front of me. "I'm going to help you."

He opens the top and tosses it in the trash and takes out an object made of black satin straps and gold buckles. Under it is a four-inch long gold bar with rounded ends like a cigar that he plucks out and tucks into his palm.

"Put this on." He hands me the strappy thing. "Buckles at the waist, this satin pad over your cunt."

He says "cunt" like a flat statement of fact, and it's more arousing than any man who'd try to make it sexy, and sits down to watch me. I have the elastic, satin, and buckles figured out in no time. It fits like a thong, with a thin satin string between my ass cheeks. The flat satin part fits over my clit and opening— and has something stiff but thin enough to be pliable inside it.

When I'm done, I stand with three tiles between my legs again so he can see me. He fiddles with the gold bar, weaving it between his fingers like a close-up magician. I'm pretty sure he's going to make it disappear and pull it from behind my ear, when he stands.

"Get in the tub. Face the window." I do it and face the one-way window to the garden. My bath is big enough for my feet to spread eighteen inches apart, and I'm pretty thrilled I've done everything right so far.

Master holds up the gold bar then presses it to my lower lip so I can feel the gentle vibration. I hope this thing goes inside me. He moves it down to my throat, then one nipple.

"Don't move," he commands. "Just listen. You're too focused on what you want, not what you need. You're going to lose it all because you're in a rush." The vibrating rod goes to the other nipple, then down my belly. "You're confused. You think patience is tolerance." He puts the rod against the satin part of the apparatus and it stays in place.

"It's a magnet," I gasp, feeling the vibrations.

Master leaves me there, moving behind me. With the little vibrating bar stuck between my legs, my clit's now at full attention. I hear the faucet go on full blast. I see him in the window's reflection, testing the temperature, fiddling with it, then turning down the flow to a minimum before plugging the drain so the tub fills. By the time he comes in front of me again, I'm breathless.

"You like it," he says.

"Yes."

"Look at you," he says, reaching for a nipple. There's a hint of something more in his voice. Appreciation, maybe? Like I've impressed him or something. He gently twists the nipple, rolling it between his fingers as if he's absorbed by it. "Keep your eyes in front of you."

I didn't know that I wasn't supposed to look at him, but okay. Face forward with the clit buzzer. Got it.

"You're going to make your husband a very happy man."

My eyes tingle. His words make me close to tears. I didn't realize it, but I'd started to doubt I could make him happy even if I got through this.

"Do you think so?" I ask. His hand drops away from my breast.

"I only say what I know or what I think. So, yes...I think so. Don't you?"

A tear falls when I blink. I hadn't intended to actually cry and thankfully, he doesn't comment on it.

"I hope so."

"I didn't ask what you hoped, but since your cunt's calling the shots at the moment, I'll take that as a yes for now."

"Thank you, Master."

"Do you want to come?"

"Yes, Master."

"Do you need to come?"

"No, Master."

He asks nothing more. He just stands there and watches as I get more and more tightly wound. The water's trickling into the tub. My thighs clench. My pussy tightens and releases. I exhale in bursts.

Then—when it's almost too much—I squeak.

"I need—" I start, but don't finish, because he pulls the gold bar away, and I lurch forward with a gulp of air.

"Get on your knees." When I kneel in the ankle-deep water, legs apart, he comes behind me again. "Bend forward. Hands on the side of the tub."

I do it, and he drops the gold bar into the water with a little splash. It bobs and spins.

"When the water rises high enough, you'll get what you need."

He spins the chair around to sit behind me and watch me in the window's reflection. But because of the dots of lights on the garden path, I can still see outside. It's late and he's here with me, making sure I make it through the program.

"Thank you, Master."

"For what?"

"You're really…"

Really what? I bow my head to think. The gold bar bounces on the surface, rippling as it vibrates. I know the physics of that exact wave pattern. How long until it reaches me and satisfies this unbearable need? Mr. Wright with his sweaty armpits and loose, wet lower lip would have made me calculate water volume in my head down to the split second.

"Head up, Juliette."

I look straight again.

"You're really making sure I do my best. I've had so many tutors, but no one's done that for me before."

"No? Are you sure?"

"My physics teacher, Mr. Wright, failed me and then called my father in to tell him. And Daddy said, 'It's your job to make sure she understands it, so do the job.' And so after that he hit my ass with a ruler whenever I did anything wrong and I saw..." I stop because Master gets up and I can see the size of the bulge in his pants.

"Go on," he says. "You saw what?"

"He had an erection when he hit me. So I made sure to get the work right because I didn't want to see that." I'm afraid he's going to think I have the same feeling about him, and I don't want him to hide it, ever. Nothing ever made me feel as good as Master's arousal. "I don't mind seeing yours, though."

The water's now halfway up my thigh. It's taking forever.

"Are you sure?"

"I like when you're hard."

The space between that admission and the next thing he says is too long, yet the water barely makes it half an inch closer.

"Good. I don't want to send you back to the Client traumatized." Another pause. I feel more than see him standing over me, watching as I wait for the gold bar to rise to my pussy. "When I'm hard from watching you, it's not for you to like or not like. It's a physical reaction from teaching you how to fuck. That's how the Client wants you finished, and my first responsibility is to him."

"I know."

"You will never belong to me."

"I understand."

"My business is built on trust and discretion, and that's the trust half." He opens his belt with a clack of the buckle. "When you make me hard, you're making the Client hard."

He sounds like he's trying to talk himself into his own philosophy, and though he may have all night to sort that out, I want to come already.

"Can you turn the water up?" I ask.

He fists his cock. I'd think the window was making it

look massive but I remember how it fit in Tammy's mouth, and the reflection is accurate. My arousal had been in a holding pattern, but now it's a gush of unmet need.

"You still have to wait to come." He strokes his length. "You have to learn the lesson."

"Okay." Deep in my chest I hum a slow tune to give myself something to focus on. He may ask me to stop, but I need it.

"Do you know why?" Slowly, he jerks off behind me, but he doesn't put an end to my humming.

"No." I pause long enough to answer, then start again. It's *Happy Birthday*, over and over.

"So you can plan a dinner party. And when the guests are there, your husband can turn to you and say, 'Go up to the bedroom, take your clothes off, lie on the bed with your legs spread,' and you'll do it." He continues stroking his cock. "And you'll wait as long as it takes until he comes upstairs with a friend from the party. They'll negotiate who gets your ass and who gets your mouth. And you'll wait while his friend inspects your mouth and asshole to see what he wants."

Master closes his eyes and exhales sharply. Every word he's saying turns me on, but that one breath makes my throbbing cunt hurt unbearably. The waterline seems like it didn't move. I'm sure I won't be able to stand another word, but Master jerks off faster and continues.

"When they tie you up, you'll wait patiently with your mouth open for your husband's cock, and you'll have a mind that can concentrate on taking it down your throat while you're getting fucked in the ass by someone else."

He comes with one grunt, spraying warm thickness onto my back and ass. Between his pleasure and the scene he described, I'm now in a mindless state of pure arousal...and the waterline isn't even close.

"And that…" he says, tucking away his beautiful dick and sitting on the chair. "…is why you need to learn patience before you meet your husband. He'll take care of you as well as I do, but he's demanding."

"I understand, Master."

I've hummed *Happy Birthday* a dozen times, but I start it over again because it's the only non-sexual thing I can concentrate on.

"You can come when the water reaches you," Master says. "Would you like me to turn the faucet up now?"

"No. I'll wait." I resume the song.

"That's the correct answer, little girl. I haven't called your father to tell him you failed. Should I?"

The question is rhetorical—not half as real as my need to come.

"It's up to you, Master," I say.

"Right again, hummingbird."

The nickname catches the next chorus in my throat. Does he not like the humming? Is it distracting for him? Am I not learning? But he'd tell me to stop if he wanted me to. He doesn't. I see him in the window's reflection, watching patiently, so I just wait for the water with his cum drying on my back.

When the water is so close I can feel its heat on my cunt, he leans over and makes a current that pushes the gold bar towards me. The floating magnet finds home, snapping against my crotch and vibrating everything under the satin.

I squeeze my eyes shut and come so hard, my entire body clenches.

When I open my eyes to thank Master, he's gone.

9

I WAKE up late in the morning. There's a message from Daddy.

"Juliette." He sounds stern for a guy Master wasn't going to call. "What's going on? You're on probation?"

I call him back but hang up before he or the voicemail picks up. Daddy won't yell at me, but he has a way of sounding disappointed that breaks me. He's only had that voice a couple of times in my life. Once, when I was about thirteen. I wasn't used to high heels. At Christmas dinner they slid out from under me and spilled Uncle Jeremy's wine. And again, at my coming-out party when he caught me alone, talking to one of the guys catering the event. Both times, his words were neutral, but the tone made me shudder.

Probation. Never in my life have I dug myself in so deep. I've never been in trouble like this before.

I call Master, but he's not in, and when the receptionist starts giving me some super-specific time to call back, I say thanks and cut the call.

I have so much on my mind and no strict, specific

instructions for what to do with my pussy or my mouth or any of the rest of me. I can spend the day by the pool eating macarons, or take off for Paris. I can do whatever I want to get my mind off my problems.

But it turns out that what I want, when it comes down to it, is to put on the Alaia dress that Master picked out for our first meeting and the black patent Louboutins that I'm really good at walking in now. I make myself up just as carefully as I do every time I go to the agency, and then have my driver take me to his office.

The receptionist, whose name I still don't know, greets me coolly. Her lipstick seems extra red today, a bold and ferocious statement on her soft, full mouth.

"I don't have an appointment," I admit. "But I'd like to see him, if I may."

"He's booked solid."

"He doesn't have ten minutes anywhere today? Like, between 9:02 and 9:12?"

"Nope." She doesn't even look at the appointment book, but she does nod towards the plush leather chairs on the opposite side of the lobby. "You can wait and see if something opens up."

"Great," I tell her. "Thank you."

As I settle in, I wish I'd brought a magazine. There aren't any out on display, and I can't quite make myself go ask the receptionist for one. Maybe it won't take that long.

The front doors open and Tammy walks through them, wearing a pale yellow dress that I recognize from Gucci's most recent runway show. It hugs her curves in all the right places, showing off the dramatic hourglass of her figure; I remember how she looked on her knees with Master's cock down her throat and feel a familiar rush of envy and jealousy.

"Juliette?" she says.

"Hi."

Last time we saw each other, things were a little tense, but today she seems thrilled to see me. In fact, she seems generally thrilled, her face lit up, her cheeks a sweet glowing pink that I also wish I had.

"Oh, I'm so happy! Master just called and told me that a spot is opening up with one of his most important clients, and my sister is up for it. Can you believe it?"

"That's..." I start, hoping I don't sound as miserably monotone as I feel. "I mean, yes! I can totally believe it! That's so wonderful. I'm so happy for her."

I'm truthful and a liar, because of course, Tammy's sister's mystery man is my husband. He has to be. This man I've been promised to—who I have always been meant for—he's moving on. He'll have another wife. She'll have everything he can give her, and I won't know what comes after for me.

It's fair, though. I don't deserve it. Waiting for the waterline to rise last night just means I earned probation instead of exile. Master came to me in the dead of night to get me a second chance.

"I guess I'll see you around," Tammy says. She nods at the receptionist and then heads back into the office, apparently so comfortable here that she no longer needs an escort.

"See you," I murmur to her retreating back.

Should I go home? Is it all already over for me?

Maybe. But also maybe not. Either way, I want to see Master and thank him for pulling me out of the abyss.

And so I sit and wait.

The morning light glides across the floors. People come and go: men in suits and a steady, endless stream of beautiful women in impossibly high heels. After a while, Tammy reappears; she waves to me on her way out the door. I wave back, and keep waiting.

The receptionist takes a lunch break, disappearing out the

front doors while a lithe, pretty boy takes over for her. I'm hungry, but the hunger doesn't seem urgent. It's just a sensation. Waiting for Master to let me orgasm was much worse than skipping lunch will be.

I don't want to get dizzy, though, so I pour myself lemon cucumber water from the carafe on the guest services table. I'm still sipping it when the receptionist returns. More clients, more in and out; the phone rings, voices chatter, I sit and sit.

The longer I sit, the more time seems to melt around me, absorbing me into it like thick, sweet honey. This is the calm I needed in Antoine's studio. It's too late now, but that is what it is. I don't feel bad about learning it late. I'm just glad I learned it in time to be a still point in the turning world.

The traffic through the lobby thins, and then stops. The receptionist gathers her things and leaves for the night. I half expect her to make me go when she does, but she doesn't even acknowledge me as she breezes out the front doors.

It's half past six, when Master finally walks out from his office. His suit is navy today. The blue picks up the green in his eyes; I glance at his throat to see if he's loosened his tie, maybe even undone a button, but he's as perfectly put together as always. He's deep in a conversation on the phone.

He nods when he sees me, but doesn't pause his stride. I nod back, still deep inside of myself as he opens the doors and walks through them. I think: *I will stay here tonight, then. I'll be here in the morning when he gets in.* Not a muscle in my body twitches. There's still nowhere else I'd rather be.

Then the doors swing open and he pokes his head through them. "You coming?" he asks.

I'm surprised that my body obeys me so easily after sitting in one position all day, but in one fluid motion, I'm on my feet, following him out the door.

THE INTERIOR OF HIS CAR, a sleek black Bugatti Chiron, cushions us from the sound of the world outside, but I can see it speeding by through the windows as he takes us out of the city, up into the hills. He drives fast and confidently, whipping us around hairpin turns, one strong hand on the gearshift, coaxing the car along. I watch his fingers on the knob and feel the phantom touch of them between my legs; I let myself imagine him reaching across and stroking me with that same lazy finesse. I could come this way, I think: the car purring beneath me, just imagining his hands working steadily between my folds.

"You don't seem nervous," he says at last.

"About what?"

"Going over a cliff."

"Being nervous is counterproductive," I tell him. "Do you know why drunk drivers survive car accidents more often than their passengers? It's because their bodies are loose, and they just roll with whatever happens. They don't try to resist it. It's people who are sober, who are panicking, who clench up and get hurt."

"Is that so?"

"Yep. I would go as loose as I could, maybe protect my head a little. Head injuries are really difficult to recover from, much more than say, a broken wrist or an arm. Once you're stable, check yourself, check your companion. Look for exit routes from the car. I'm small enough to get out through the windows. You might not be so lucky."

"And then what?"

"Well, depends on how the car is doing. But if I can, I drive home."

"You can drive stick?"

"I test drove a concept car for Lexus at Tsukuba Race-track last year. It had a manual transmission."

"What did you think of the car?"

"It was fast...but a little loose on the curves."

He swings off the road and into a little overlook with a sprawling and glittering view of the city. The sun is just about to finish setting, and the sky is ablaze with color, gorgeous pink light filling up the car with a soft, almost ethereal glow.

"This is nice," I say. Then, because it is, I wish I could forget everything going on and just pretend we're the only two people in the world.

"It is," he says.

But I can't pretend forever. He hasn't told me about the probation yet, and it's not like him to shy away from anything—especially not bad news.

"Why did you bring me here?"

"Well." He keeps his eyes focused on the brilliant scenery. "I'm here because this is how I like to end my days. I work hard, as you know, and life in the office can be a bit...stress-ful. I take a moment to remember how much bigger the world is than my problems." He pauses, then says, "I have no idea why *you're* here though."

Weird. I just assumed he had a plan for me, the way he's always had plans for me before.

"I'm here because you told me to get in the car."

"Why were you waiting in my office all day, Juliette?" he asks.

It occurs to me that this might be the last time we talk, but it also might be our first real conversation. Always before there was a script I felt like I was supposed to be following—like he knew what answer he wanted from me even before I spoke. Now neither of us knows what happens next. For once, we're on even ground, and it feels nice. I take a moment to appreciate being alone with him—just us in this small, quiet, intimate space, the world spread out in front of us, before I respond.

"I waited all day to ask you why I'm on probation," I say. "But I guess I know already. If I don't belong to your client anymore, you have to find me another husband while I'm still a virgin."

Master's expression doesn't change. "You waited all day to just ask me what you already know?"

I should have cried myself out of tears last night, but they sting at my eyes all the same. I hate letting him down. I hate it so much. "I need to hear you say it!" I exclaim.

"You're in a holding pattern while we plan your next lesson."

"A holding pattern? You, of all people, resorting to euphemisms?"

He laughs.

Have I ever heard him laugh before?

It's like cathedral bells. Every bird in the world singing at once. Like every birthday and Christmas in a whole lifetime happening at once.

"It's not a euphemism." He looks at the view of the setting sun.

"If you won't call it probation to save my feelings, then it is."

He looks at me. "Maybe 'probation' is the euphemism, hummingbird."

"Whatever. It's still probation."

"The important thing is that you learn the lessons."

"I can't keep failing. I can't do it anymore. Not to me, and not to you."

"You can't?" he asks. "Tell me, how did you feel today, waiting for me?

How did I feel? "I felt," I start to say, before I even really know the answer. "At first I felt annoyed. But then I discovered the people coming in and out of the office were interesting, and that entertained me for a while." I think about the watching I did, and how it melted, at some point, into something else. Something calmer. "And then I just. I don't know. I felt peaceful. There was a rhythm in it. Waiting. And then the afternoon flew by."

"And this is you *failing* at patience?"

For one startling second, everything seems clear. He's right. I can be patient. I was present all day today in a way I never was for Antoine; I could do that again, now that I know how to access it. I can be patient with Master. I can be patient with myself. I can finish the lessons and get everything I ever wanted.

Master basically taught me the lesson last night and then put me on probation today, only to tell me it's not a big deal. He's never going to let me get on an even footing. He's keeping me insecure that I'll ever be able to mold myself to his liking…because he's never going to tell me what he needs me to be. He's going to continue to treat me like a child who can't handle the whole picture of who his client is and what he wants.

My conversation with Jane echoes in my mind: why won't men just tell us what they want, instead of asking us to play their games without ever explaining the rules? If I understood what was going to happen next, I wouldn't have to be anxious and impatient. If my future wasn't always in question, maybe I could really relax and enjoy myself.

"Are you going to tell me what's next?"

"Not yet."

"Of course."

All my life I've done as I was told, whether or not I understood the reasons. I'm done living that way. To prove it, I swing the car door open, get out, and start walking down the mountain. It'll take me hours to get home.

Good thing I know so much about patience.

I am going to walk these shoes through.

I haven't gotten very far when I hear the car's engine start up then the sound of asphalt under tires. I expect Master to whizz by me in a cloud of diesel and rubber, to leave me to my long, lonely walk.

Instead, he idles alongside me with the car in neutral to keep pace with my high-heeled feet as they pick out step after step after step.

He rolls a window down and shouts, "Get in."

"I don't have to be obedient anymore. And you don't have to even talk to me or take care of me, either," I remind him. He owes me nothing. I owe him nothing. Can't he just leave me alone?

"It's not safe walking on the side of the road, Juliette."

Of course I know that. This road is just two thin lanes, no guardrail. Which one of us just described how to survive a car crash? I'm intimately aware of the danger I'm facing, but at least I'm choosing to face it. "Can you just let me live with my mistakes, please?" I ask.

"Yes. I certainly will, when it's time. But for now, you need to get into the car before some idiot runs you off the road."

Master's voice is firm and commanding, and, as always, it goes straight to my pussy. More than that, though, he's right, and I don't want to die just to prove a point.

What seals it, though, is that when I glance over at his face, he looks almost pleading, like he actually cares about what happens to me, and I can't let him suffer with worry.

I stop walking, and he stops the car. I climb back into the passenger seat; as soon as the door slams behind me, he's speeding us down the mountain, as if he doesn't want to give me time to change my mind.

"Antoine called," he says. "This afternoon. Apparently, he hates failing as much as you do."

Of course he didn't tell me, because the lesson is the important thing.

"I hope you told him I'm sorry I was such a shitty model."

Master ignores me. "He has an idea for you," he says.

"An idea? What kind of idea?"

"Patience, Juliette. Patience."

Master smirks at me, reaching for the gearshift as he swings us smoothly around another breathtaking turn.

10

I DON'T FIND out about Antoine's idea until the following morning, of course, when I get a call to go to the studio immediately. Because, patience is virtuous but punctuality is professionalism.

When I arrive, I have to force myself to stay serene when I discover both Antoine and Master are there, waiting to decide my fate.

"Strip, *cherie*," Antoine demands without even saying hello, and I obey—skimming out of my plain, simple outfit. No more fancy gold lingerie, no more black silk, short skirts, and tight dresses.

"It occurred to me when she got up from kneeling," Antoine says to Master as I step out of my underwear. "I saw the paint on her knees and thought—ah, yes. She was never meant to be a portrait. She herself must be the work. I will display my talents on her skin; my brush will worship every inch of her, and the results will be sublime. Imagine that body, covered in paint. She will be art. I will make sure of it."

He snaps his fingers in my direction and commands: "Kneel."

I do, realizing he's right. This isn't about me dressing up in a costume. This is about letting his inspiration adorn me. There's no fear or shame in being naked in front of these men. I am the art. I relish the heat of Master's gaze on my body, imagining his hands going everywhere his eyes touch: cupping my breasts and tweaking my nipples, smoothing down my stomach and slipping between my legs.

"She loves to be looked at," Antoine murmurs, eyeing the way my nipples are already hard for him, goosebumps breaking out on my skin. "The process will be part of the work." He stands beside me and touches the hollow of my throat, where I'm sure he can feel my quickening pulse. "We'll start here, emphasizing her long, graceful neck." His fingers trail across my shoulder. "She dances, yes?"

"Up until just recently."

"*Bon*. Fifth position." When I raise them, he draws his finger over the line of my arms.

"The colors will draw the eye out, out, to the palms of her hands." My body lights up everywhere he touches me; I feel as sensitive as the first time Master spanked me, every nerve ending lit up and begging for more. "Rise for us." I rise gracefully, arms still extended. Antoine's touch remains maddeningly light and steady as he describes the lilies he'll paint across my shoulder blades, the way he'll define my waist and trace my legs, his hands following the path his voice describes. My body like an object while his hands remind me of just how much it can feel.

"But the focus of the energy, of course, will come right from where she herself puts it." He cups between my legs. "Her cunt."

I groan at the sudden sensation.

"So reactive," he says. "It's remarkable, no?"

"Indeed," Master rumbles, and the sound of his voice, the

knowledge that he's still here, looking at me, a steady, maddening pressure against my swollen clit.

"Every inch of her will be covered." A hand slips down my back, parting my cheeks, ghosting over my hole. "Every inch," he emphasizes, "will be art."

Antoine drops to his knees in front of me.

"Juliette," Master says, and I know instantly what he wants. I kick my feet eighteen inches apart.

Antoine strokes his fingers up my thighs and finally, finally, against my seam, where he can feel how wet I am from all of his teasing. "We can photograph it, and we will, but that's just a document. The nature of the work is temporary." Then he nudges me open and pinches my clit. "This will be permanent," he says. "Such a little jewel deserves its own adornment. I have custom-made a piercing that will highlight her perfect cunt, and make sure no one misses that every part of her has been given in service of my work."

He stands back up again, and though I've done nothing but hold still for the last ten minutes, I'm breathing hard, and I'm hot all over, prickly with desire and need.

Patience, I remind myself. Then I wait to hear what Master says. The paint is one thing, but the piercing—won't his client mind?

Apparently not. "I approve," he says. "The client wants you to follow your vision to the fullest. Can you begin tomorrow?"

Antoine nods. "We will need to show it immediately."

"I'll make arrangements." With that, Master nods his head decisively. "I'll see you tomorrow, then." And my heart flutters in my chest, its beat pulsing all the way down to my pussy with excitement. He's going to be here to watch me, which will only make it more difficult, and more thrilling, too.

11

THE NEXT MORNING, I wake with my hand between my legs and realize it's the last time I'll feel my clit unpierced. Last night, I read that they create a sweet, constant pressure against the clit that can all too easily spill over into genuine need. I imagine my husband's strong fingers tugging on it, his tongue flicking at it, and get out of bed and into the shower before I get too aroused to help myself.

When I get out of the shower, I go into the kitchen to make myself one last snack before I brush my teeth and head out. Jane is there, of course, having anticipated me, like she always does: she points to a plate of water crackers and goat cheese and grins at me. "Can't have your belly rumbling while you're being art," she says.

"Thank you." I take the plate and sit down, settling my plush bathrobe carefully around me. "Are you going to be here when I come home tonight?"

"Do you need me?"

I do want someone to come home to in case the piercing hurts or everything goes wrong, but she never asks things like that. She anticipates what I want. So there must be a reason she asked.

"I think I might want to be alone."

This is a big fat lie, but it's the only way to get the truth out of her.

"Okay, that works out, then. I'm seeing Bruce tonight."

"Oh are you!"

"I am." Her face is flushed with happiness, and it's nice to see my friend so excited about something. "I really think... I really think tonight is it, Juliette. He's going to fuck me. God, I can't wait." Her voice drops when she says, "I've been wet for him all day."

"I know the feeling."

"I can't wait to hear about tonight. All the rich men in fancy suits looking at you."

She's right: the room will be full of rich men in fancy suits tonight, and one of them could be my husband.

Maybe tonight is the night I recognize him, or he introduces himself to me. Buys the art my body has come. Maybe tonight is the night I find out, finally, after all my patient waiting, who he actually is.

Worse, though, the probation may mean he's not going to be there tonight or ever again.

I ARRIVE at the studio completely naked under a silk robe, my hair swept into a neat bun and my face clean of makeup for the first time in a long, long time. I'm a perfect canvas, blank and ready for whatever Antoine has in store. I'm not focusing on the promise of the husband who ordered this and who I may have lost already. For today, I'm not invested in some eventual future. I'm just present in the now of our interaction, savoring the sensation of the morning sun on my bare skin as I stand naked in the middle of the studio.

Antoine has me sit on the same pedestal as always, but this time there's no seductive posing, just my legs spread and my arms at my sides. "Hold still," he instructs, and measures every bit of my body with his eyes.

It's easier, now that I've done it once, to slip into waiting: letting time rush over me like water, feeling no need to do anything but be carried along by its current. Master arrives and doesn't say anything; he goes over to a corner and takes some papers from his briefcase, which he reads quietly. Antoine's housekeeper brings him coffee, which he sips while he works. His presence settles me and makes me feel even more secure in what I'm doing. I can do anything as long as Master is here with me while I do it.

"You need to go to the bathroom now, before it's not possible."

When I return, Antoine's holding a small silver egg in one hand and a remote control in the other. "This may not be a portrait, but it's still about sex," he says. "I need to feel desire in your body while I work—that's what will make it come alive. So while I sketch, this will be inside of you. It will provide the ultimate combination of stillness and action."

Having Master's powerful body in the room with my vulnerable naked one makes it easy for Antoine to slip the egg into my cunt. It's cool and heavy inside of me, a welcome pressure where I've wanted one for so long. He presses the remote control button, and a warm, gentle buzzing begins, setting up a steady, coaxing rhythm that makes me want to clench down and writhe, get my fingers on my clit and rub myself until I come. Instead, I hold still.

"You will be allowed to come," he says, pointing to a small clock set on the table where Master works. "But only when the alarm goes off."

I can't see when it's set for, so I have no idea how long I have to hold on. Antoine presses another button and the steady buzz inside of me changes to a pulsing rhythm.

"Until then," he continues. "Do not move. Do not breathe hard. You are not a statue, but you will do your best to act like one. Yes?"

"Yes."

"I have the air conditioning set to keep you from sweating." He brushes my hard nipple with the backs of his fingers, illustrating the effect of the cold air."

And we begin.

Antoine torments me with his brush, touching me everywhere and yet never giving me enough. Master is always there, but rarely pays attention to me; sometimes he takes calls, blithely discussing business or inviting guests to the studio that night, while I try not to come from the combination of the buzzing in my cunt and the sound of his voice in the air. I restrain myself while Antoine drags the brush along my inner thighs, blowing to dry the paint.

It's worse when I bend over, hands reaching behind. Master's on the phone, eye to eye with me, all of his intensity directed at me as I let Antoine paint between my ass cheeks.

The alarm goes off at lunchtime when Antoine puts his brushes away.

"You may stand," he says. "The outlines are set. Look at yourself."

In the mirror, I'm covered in thin black outlines, like a three-dimensional sketch pad. Suddenly the egg's vibration in my cunt doubles, and my knees get weak. Master comes into the reflection with the remote control in his hand.

"Did you forget?" he asks.

The constant arousal had become pleasurable white noise —a part of my existence and not something to rub to climax or wish away.

I don't have to answer. He smiles and presses a button. The egg pulses, and I can barely hold myself up for the earth-shattering orgasm.

NAKED AND ON my feet to keep from disturbing the paint, I eat. I try to take a bathroom break without touching too much of myself. When I return, there's no clock on the table and the egg isn't reintroduced. Antoine's put two boxes in front of the pedestal, and a muscular man in a tight T-shirt is sitting by it, cleaning metal instruments.

The last time I got anything pierced it was my ears, and I was ten years old. I have no idea what to expect. I can't help being scared.

"Sit," Antoine says. "Spread your legs for Rusty like a good girl."

Rusty's a little rough around the edges, chewing gum on one side of his mouth as he puts each of my feet on the boxes. I catch sight of the tray of implements that looks like what you'd see at the dentist. The porcelain ring designed for me, with a thin gold metal rod where the piercing will pass through the hood of my clit, sits in the center of another tray. It's beautiful—delicate and gleaming under the studio's bright lights. I picture it nestled in my folds, circling my nub, and feel a wave of satisfaction.

To my surprise, Master puts down what he's been doing to come watch. I had thought he would ignore this part the way he ignored the others—but he draws close as Antoine describes to Rusty what he wants.

Is he interested in my pain, I wonder? Is this what he wants to see from me? Is he curious how I'll handle it?

Is it possible he's protecting me, making sure nothing goes wrong?

"I got it." Rusty yanks my delicate folds like he's not concerned with the woman attached to them. "Easy enough." With a "huh" of curiosity he sticks a finger inside, then removes it.

"Fucking virgin, is she?"

"Her choice," Master says, and it's got a little bit of menace in it. Like he doesn't want this guy commenting on my hymen.

"Whatever you say, boss," Rusty says, fiddling and disinfecting his tools. They clink together and the alcohol stings my nose. They look sharp, and I'm suddenly frightened.

"Juliette," Master says. "Pop quiz."

What? Now? How am I expected to concentrate? Does he want me to be reciting the periodic table while Rusty slides a needle through the hood of my clit?

"What year," he starts, thinks, then finishes the question. "Was the first Wimbledon Championship held?"

"1877," I say. I played on those courts a handful of times, when I was still a teenager. My instructor was a seeded French player and one of my first crushes; no wonder Antoine's accent makes me so weak.

"Who is the current prime minister of Belgium?"

"Alexander de Croo." We had dinner with him when we were there last winter; my father let me wear one of my mother's old furs, and it was the most like a woman I had ever felt. He never lets me touch her things, so it meant everything to me that he believed I was worthy of it.

"Other than Yves Klein blue, what other colors have been copyrighted?"

Before I can answer, Antoine says, "Deep breath in," and I understand what the point of this was: to distract me so I couldn't freeze up while he was getting ready. I lock eyes with Master.

"Tiffany Blue. Owens Corning Pink. Barbie Pink."

Rusty leans down between my legs and sprays something tingly on me, and my clit goes numb.

"Caterpillar Yellow."

He pulls the hood of my clit. It's coming, and it's going to hurt.

"You missed a pink," Master says. "Darker."

"T-Mobile Pink. Um…"

"Go on."

"UPS Brown. Sanka Or—"

The pain is brief but sharp, starting as a sting between my legs and then radiates outward as a hard throbbing stab as my shocked body tries to figure out what just happened. I hold still as Rusty threads the piercing through and then secures it in place, trying to control my breathing.

"Orange. Louboutin R—"

My face contorts in a denial that anything hurts, but I can't help the tears that slips through and slide down my cheek. Then—a moment later—the pain recedes and I can think clearly again.

"Red."

I drop back, legs still spread and take a deep breath.

"You're smearing your paint," Master murmurs, carefully patting my cheek dry with a handkerchief he's pulled from his pocket. The material is soft against me, and I let myself drown in the tenderness of this brief touch. "I want my Client to see your perfection."

He's already taking a call on the other side of the studio when I realize what his words portend.

12

THE PHOTOGRAPHER ARRIVES HALF an hour before the guests. Antoine places my body where he wants it and makes careful adjustments. When he steps away to let the photographer do her work, I'm bent over the pedestal I used to sit on, leaning on my weight on my hands, my legs spread so that the work he's done between my cheeks and on my inner thighs is visible. Beneath my feet there's a cold, slick mirror, which reflects my cunt with its pierced clit.

It has to be this way so that they can see: every part of me is art. Antoine's brush has visited my armpits and elbows, has stroked my crack and tickled my hole. My spine is a long line of color. Even the undersides of my feet are painted. The photographer documents every inch of me with a whirr and a click.

I hold still, completely on display, as the audience filters in. It's another group of men, more dark suits and handsome faces; their voices are a low rumble in the room, and the sense of masculine power is intoxicating. It's exciting to watch them watch me, but I try to stay peaceful, to sink into the calm of waiting, so that when my husband sees me, he'll only see placid ease on my face. The only place I want to be is where I am.

It gets harder as the night goes on, though. The time between camera clicks grows, then the pictures stop altogether. My arms get tired, and so do my legs. My feet hurt and my pussy is wet, swollen, excited by the attention and ready for more of it even though nothing comes. The men who surround me can see it in the mirror, and I watch their hungry gazes trace the lines of my folds, catching on the glisten of white that circles my clit.

They eventually break into their own conversations, and I am no more than pretty furniture.

Antoine lets a few of the men touch me, asking me to put one leg up on the pedestal so they could inspect the clit ring more closely. Their breath blows against me as they discuss the art of Antoine's creation, treating me like I was just another object in the room.

But I'm not an object, and so, finally, when the last guest has filtered out, I stand up and stretch out my sore muscles, look around and find I'm alone.

No guests. No photographer. No Antoine. No Master.

No husband.

13

WHEN I WAKE, it's to Jane knocking on my bedroom door. I open it to find her dressed already, carrying a silver tray that's laid with my favorite breakfast: a carafe of coffee, the glistening sections of an orange, and a basket of rolls so fresh I can see steam rising from under the white linen napkin that covers them. "I didn't want to wake you," she says. "But it's nearly ten, so..."

"No, thank you. I appreciate it." I go to sit at the small table in my room, noting where I'm still sore from holding myself in place last night, the flecks of paint that linger around my cuticles and in the crease of my elbow. They escaped last night's shower but won't get away today.

Jane sets the tray down before taking a seat in the other chair.

"How was the show?" she asks.

I pour myself coffee. "Fine," I say. "I mean, it went well. I held my pose; I did everything Antoine asked of me. I was patient, and I was obedient. It looked incredible. People were really excited about it; I heard someone telling Antoine it was a breakthrough in his work."

I pause to butter one of the rolls, and Jane hears what I'm not saying.

"But you didn't meet him."

I shake my head. "Another lesson in patience, I guess."

"Oh Juliette. I'm so sorry."

"No, I'm sorry. That means you have to wait, too."

"It's all right. These rolls are pretty good!"

I can tell she doesn't want to dwell. "What about you?" I ask. "Please tell me he finally gave in to you. He had to, right? Oh, tell me he did!"

It's Jane's turn to shake her head. I must look despondent, because she laughs. "It wasn't all bad," she says. "We went to his place and watched a movie together. I thought I would explode from just being near him—he's so big all over, and I wanted him to touch me so badly. I was wet before he even opened the door. At first I thought he was going to ignore me, just let me sit there on the couch next to him all night— but finally he reached over and pulled me into his lap."

My breath quickens, imagining what it would feel like to have a man pressed against my back, my body surrounded by his, at his mercy in the dark.

"He touched me," Jane continues, her voice dropping at the memory. "Put his hands under my shirt, and his calluses were rough against my skin, but I didn't mind. He cupped my breasts and pinched my nipples, and I—I got distracted." She's blushing, now, at what she's saying or the heat of the memory or both.

"He—he told me to keep my eyes on the screen. And then he put his hand between my legs and…" Jane trails off, but the pink in her cheeks tells the rest of the story for her.

"Did he let you come?"

She nods. "It felt incredible," she says. "He got me off with his fingers inside of me, and they were so thick. I felt full. I wanted more."

"But?"

"But he wouldn't let me."

"At all?"

"When I was done, he told me to turn around—the movie was over by then anyway, though I couldn't tell you anything that happened after he started touching me. He pulled himself out and let me touch him, but just with my hands."

"Is he…"

"So big," Jane says. "I almost couldn't believe it."

I flash back to Master's bruiser of an erection, and a wave of want washes over me. I sucked Antoine's dick so many times in his studio, let him come on my face and my breasts, but I still want to know what Master would feel like, how much bigger he would be as he fucked my throat and pulled my hair.

"But he wouldn't let you fuck him."

"No. I asked, after, but he said… he said he was too rough for me. That he was afraid he'd hurt me. That he *cared* about me too much. If he cares about me, though, why won't he give me what I want?"

"I don't know. I don't understand anything men do." That's certainly true: I don't understand Bruce. I barely understand Antoine, or Master. I get that my husband wants me trained, but part of me still can't accept that he won't do the training himself. That he doesn't mind that I've made myself come for other men, that I trained my throat to swallow another man's cock before I'd ever taken his. That more and more, when I imagine my first time, it isn't my husband's face I see, but Master's sharp green eyes and sensuous mouth, his strong body pinning me in place as he fucks me open and watches how perfectly I can swallow him down.

This can't be what my husband wants, yet it is. It has to be.

"Oh, I almost forgot," Jane says. "There's a note for you." She pulls a white envelope from her pocket and hands it to me, and when I recognize the expensive paper, my heart leaps with anticipation.

The card says one word.

NOW

"I'm sorry," I say to Jane when I look up. "But—"

"It's fine! I'll clear this—do you want anything else before you leave?"

I shake my head. "I'm fine," I say. "Thank you, though. And we'll talk more about all of this when I get back. We'll figure it out, I promise. I'll make sure of it."

Jane smiles at me, as radiant as the sun. "Thank you," she says, before standing to take the tray. "You're a good friend, Juliette." Her praise means almost as much to me as Master's does.

———

MASTER IS SITTING behind his desk when I arrive. His expression is almost as blank as usual, but there's a hint of a smile that warms my entire body.

"You did well last night," he says.

"I loved it," I say honestly. "Antoine did such gorgeous work on me, and so I felt beautiful. I felt worthy of everyone's attention, even though I felt really vulnerable, too."

"I could tell how much you liked it," Master says, and my pussy twitches at the thought of him seeing how wet I was, how much I loved being put on display like that. The clit ring nestled in my folds is a more welcome pressure every day, and before I can stop myself, I imagine him teasing it with his fingertips, making me moan.

"The only thing…" I say, and then pause. Maybe I shouldn't complain.

"The only thing," Master prompts, though, so I continue.

"The only thing is...did my husband buy the photographs?"

"Maybe." Master shrugs. "Maybe not. Why does it matter?"

"Since my body was the art, that's the only record of this lesson happening. I thought he'd want to own it for a memento."

Master's grin exists for only a moment at the edges of his mouth. "What about you doesn't he already own, Juliette?"

The words pulse through my body like a heartbeat. The truth is, I would do anything Master asked if he said it like that. But Master is not my husband.

"I'm glad he'll still have my virginity," I say. "Something I can give to him and him alone."

"Who says that he will?"

I'm genuinely startled. "What do you mean? Of course he will. I've been saving myself for him. *Patiently.*" Wasn't that the point of the lesson? Have I misunderstood this all *again*?

"If he chooses for you to not wait, then you won't," Master says.

"But..." I don't even have words for how ridiculous this is. Weeks and weeks spent learning patience and the point was to learn how *not* to wait?

"He doesn't want an awkward, inexperienced virgin," Master says. "He wants a woman who knows how to please him. Do you want to be that woman, or are you going to freeze up again?"

"Well, I'm not going to fail." I've worked too hard for this my whole life. I will succeed on whatever terms Master and my husband require.

I just don't know how to feel about the rest of it. Until recently, no man had ever touched me intimately; I've gotten used to being naked in front of strangers, to my tutors' hands on me. I've had Antoine's cock down my throat so often I know the taste of him by heart. But I balanced all of it with the thought that I was saving something—that there would be one way in which my husband would know me that no one else had.

"Go home and think about it," Master says, but his voice isn't cruel. He sounds kind, and I bask in that like a kitten in the sun. "Be back here at 9:07 tomorrow morning if you're ready for a man to finally fuck you."

Again, I am dismissed.

Master Class continues with Lesson Three: Take

I thought my third lesson would be easier.
I was wrong.
M says I need to learn to take pleasure.
He thinks studying under Jackson will train me.
But my thoughts are uncontrollable.
And so are my fantasies...

Get Take

TAKE

I thought my third lesson would be easier.
I was wrong.
M says I need to learn to take pleasure.
He thinks studying under Jackson will train me.
But my thoughts are uncontrollable.
And so are my fantasies…

1

When I walk into the reception area of Master's office, I'm smiling. The skirt of my Oscar de la Renta dress is full enough to be girly, but short enough to be suggestive, especially since underneath it I'm wearing a set of lacy cream-colored La Perla underwear that sets off my tan. I can't help imagining Master's eyes rising from the tips of my high-heeled pumps to the hem of the skirt. The thought settles hot between my legs as I announce myself to the receptionist, and I'm unbearably aware of the little ring that circles my hood and underlines my pleasure: a gift from my last tutor, a constant reminder of all I'm learning, and all I have yet to learn.

The second hand on my Rolex ticks over, marking the minute at 9:07 a.m., which means I am exactly on time.

Not that I expect to be seen right away; after the time I spent learning patience and obedience under Master's tutelage, I've gotten used to operating on other people's schedules. But the receptionist responds to my name with a simple, "He'll see you now," and a nod in the direction of Master's office. "Go ahead," she says.

I practically float down the hallway. The first few times I was here I was awed by this place, and though it's still beautiful, with a fresh vase of lilies sitting in a shaft of sunlight on a perfectly placed end table, it feels more and more familiar every time. Maybe I've proven myself enough that I can feel like I belong here now? It feels dangerous to even consider, and yet, also delicious.

This is the place where I come for instructions in the erotic finishing my husband-to-be has commanded me to undergo, where Master molds me into the woman he wants me to be. I've never met my intended, but if Master is anything to go by, he has very exacting tastes. So far I've struggled, but this morning, bolstered by my recent success as Antoine's model, I'm feeling confident that I can handle whatever gets thrown my way.

I still get nervous when I see him though; I don't think I'll ever not react to Master's presence in a room. He's tall, first of all, and broad-shouldered, with a commanding and powerful silhouette. But it's not just that. It's the way he holds that body, the way that, even now when he's standing by the window flipping through a sheaf of papers, he looks more coolly in control during his thoughtless, casual moments than most men ever do their entire lives. When he turns his gaze on me, the intensity in his vivid green eyes goes straight below my waist. My tiny piercing is definitely more snug now than it was when I walked into the building, and we both know it.

I stand with my feet exactly eighteen inches apart, hands at my sides, awaiting his instructions.

I expect him to ignore me. That's our usual routine: he continues with what he's doing until he's done, leaving me to maintain my position and keep myself from fidgeting, from complaining, from feeling too exposed, standing here at his mercy in my damp panties, my nipples visible underneath the thin silk of my dress.

Instead, he snaps off his glasses and closes the file of papers he's been going through. "Sit," he says, nodding at a chair.

I sit in the chair in front of his desk, but he doesn't sit behind it.

As ever, he's wearing an impeccably tailored dark suit, shirt done up to the top collar button, tie meticulously wound into a double Windsor. What I wouldn't give just to see the shape of the arms stretching his sleeves, but he's not mine to want, I have to remind myself, and I will never be his to have. He's only preparing me for my husband, acting as his proxy. He's an intermediary, not my ultimate goal.

Some days, though it's hard not to wish he wasn't quite so good at his job.

"Most of the candidates I mentor don't make it to this point," Master says. "You're a very lucky young lady." He doesn't sound proud of me, though, and he's barely looking at me, like the existence of this praise is supposed to be enough to convince me that he means it.

Unfortunately, that works. I've known Master long enough to know that he doesn't say nice things unless I've really and truly earned them. In fact, I'm so busy basking that it takes me a moment to really understand what he just said. *Luck.* I'm not lucky. I've been an excellent student my whole life; I've worked incredibly hard at all of my tutoring before this, and every lesson he and my instructors have given me since I started with him. Luck has nothing to do with it.

But I'm smart enough not to start that argument now.

"Congratulations," he intones.

And for a second, my heart beats with wild, joyful hope. Does that mean we're done? I've graduated? I've passed my tests?

"You're out of probation," Master continues. "You'll be allowed to continue training."

Oh. I suppose a few weeks ago, when I did almost fail out of the program, I might have been more excited, but after having glimpsed what I thought was an ending, it just feels like more of the same. I can't keep the disappointment out of my voice when I say, "Great."

I expect him to admonish me for my attitude, but Master is still looking somewhere over my right shoulder, cold and impervious as a sleek black sports car, rain beading up on its perfectly waxed exterior. With every beat of my heart, I wish he would open himself up and let me climb inside.

"First, though"—his eyes snap back to me— "there's a matter between us that needs to be addressed."

I can think of about a million questions I want answered, but I pass the identity of my future husband and go for the second most obvious one. "The fact that I don't even know your name?"

"No." Master has been standing, the contrast between the size of his body and mine made more pronounced by our positions, but he pulls out his chair and takes a seat before he says, "In my work here, it's crucial that I remain professional with the candidates. My detachment from you keeps the Client first in my mind. It's is part of the package, and it's something I'm very proud of."

"Okay." I mean, I could have guessed that; Master is so distant and professional with me that it aches. But this is the first time he's ever willingly said *anything* about himself to me, and I want to encourage that, so I ask, "So you're not going to tell me your name?"

He ignores the jibe, just like he always does. "The other night, I invited you into my car and drove you to a place that's personal to me."

Oh, I remember. Speaking of sleek little sports cars. It

was the night I thought I was out of the program forever; Master drove us up the side of a mountain, took every turn without touching the brake, and the sight of his hands, strong and capable, deft and certain, on the car's gearshift were almost enough to make me come untouched. He goes up there to put things in perspective, he told me: to remind himself that the work he does at this office is a part of his life, but not the whole of it. We sat and watched the sunset together, and I think it was the longest he's ever gone without telling me to strip or kneel. "It was nice," I remind him.

"It was a mistake, and I apologize for it," he says.

Oh. Oh. Okay.

I wonder if it's like this with all of Master's clients, though. How could a woman meet him and not want him? How could she go through all of this erotic torment, imagining her husband but not meeting him, always turned on but rarely allowed to get off, and not be desperate for him—not think to herself, *I hope his client is just like him?*

I wonder how many of his trainees have gotten to ride in his car. It sounds like not that many, and I cling to the intimacy of the memory, the knowledge that I have one tiny piece of him that they don't. It feels more precious than any gift I've been given—my Hermes scarves and diamond bracelets, or even the yacht Daddy named after me on my eighteenth birthday. Anyone could have bought me those things; Master's attention is something I earned.

Master says, "I've spoken to the Client about the indiscretion. He's not pleased; it will remain a mark against me. Not you. And it won't happen again."

I can't bear the thought of Master in trouble, especially not because of me. "But it's fine," I remind him. We just sat in the car and looked at the sunset; in fact, after that brief period of peace, we did fight. I jumped out of the car and tried to walk down the mountain in stilettos. The only threat to my husband was in my traitorous heart, and it's as bad now, in this office, as it was when we were together on that mountaintop. If there's a problem here, it's me, not him. "Did you tell him nothing happened? I can vouch for you."

"*Nothing happened,*" Master repeats. A small, private smile steals over his features, and even if I don't get the joke, I love watching his mouth move. "Nothing happened. You're right, and yet, you miss the point. Again. But it's to be expected, even from such an excellent student."

This is the most confusing visit to Master's office ever. After a month of learning patience, he doesn't make me wait; he apologizes for something I enjoyed, calls me excellent, and then says I've missed the point of something important. I don't know whether to sulk or to beam, to thank him or to apologize.

He saves me the trouble by taking a card out of his pocket and placing it on the desk in front of him.

"Your next lesson," he says. "Take it."

So I do. The heavy white cardstock reads only *Jackson Palmer - Sexual Practitioner* and when I see it, I can't help myself: I laugh.

"Sexual practitioner?" I ask, looking up to see if Master thinks this is funny, too. "That's a guy who has sex? He needs a card for that?"

Master is unamused. "You're set up for morning, two days from now. He's going to teach you how to fuck," he says.

"He's going to show me porn?"

"No," Master says. "He's going to fuck you until you're good at it." I love the way he says *fuck*: the rumble of his voice shaping around the sounds of the word feels like stubble scraping against my skin, a slap across my ass: pain and pleasure, plain and dirty, short and brusque and to the point.

I'm so distracted by it that I can't believe I just heard what I heard. "What?" I ask.

"You heard me."

Master looks like he's getting ready to dismiss me, so I yelp out, "Wait! I'm a virgin."

"You've mentioned that."

Of course I have, but...but...

"For my husband," I say. "The Client." I invoke the title of the man who has all the power in this room anyway, as if trying to call him down from heaven. "I mean, that's the point, isn't it? He's my first?"

"If it was the point, would I be sending you there?" Master asks, his voice as bored and flat as I've ever heard it. "No. I wouldn't. So either you trust the process or you don't, but with or without you, the process will continue. Do you understand?"

I do. I hate it, but I do, and so I nod once, not trusting myself to sound polite if I respond verbally.

"Good. My receptionist will give you the details on your birth control appointment. Meeting over," Master says, and he stands again, turning his back to me so that he can re-open his folder and start flipping through his stupid papers again. I'm not about to get dinged for disobedience, so I head out of the office, feeling far less sure of myself than when I walked in.

2

"I'M JUST NOT sure what to do."

My companion, Jane, has heard this refrain from me at least a thousand times by now; she's had to sit through so much of my complaining and uncertainty as my training has unfolded. As ever, though, she bears it with grace, her head tilted back as a bead of sweat runs from her temple across her rosy cheek, down her neck and between her breasts. Apart from the two of us, the sauna at Les Bains is blessedly empty, which means I can speak freely while we sweat. I shift from side to side, unsealing the backs of my legs from the damp cedarwood underneath them, before I continue.

"This Palmer guy—Master said he was going to fuck me, and it sounded pretty...pretty clear when he said it, but I still can't believe it. I'm a virgin. In this day and age, an actual virgin. I've preserved my purity my whole life. I've never heard of a man who *wanted* a woman who'd been—who'd been used before. By other men." My education has covered so much—quantum mechanics, ancient Latin, how to write a sonnet and sharpen a knife—but somehow, it's left me completely unprepared for this situation. What am I missing? How can I make myself understand what's going on here?

"Maybe," Jane says, "he wants to make sure you like it?"

That doesn't make any sense. If my husband wants to know if I'm interested in sex, all he has to do is look at how turned on I get in Master's presence, how I came for Antoine in his studio over and over again, swallowed his cock and begged for more. "I'm going to like it, trust me, I can tell," I say. "Especially with the right guy, I'm sure it's going to be great. But it's like *he* doesn't trust it, and now my wedding night won't be special." I hate to think of my husband doubting me, and even more than that, I hate to think of his doubt taking something special from between us.

"It will be," Jane assures me. "And honestly, I think it's kind of nice you're not being thrust into this whole wedding night situation with no idea what to expect."

That's fair enough. I can't help envying Jane just a little bit, though—she's been seeing our estate's caretaker, Bruce, and that situation seems so much less complicated for her than Master and my tutors are for me. Of course, Bruce refuses to fuck her, so I can understand why she'd prefer to be in my shoes. We've been slowly sharing these kinds of confidences with each other, and I'm so grateful to have her by my side as we both explore this part of our lives together. Jane's been my companion almost my entire life; my family pays her for her work, but she's also my closest friend.

Well, maybe my only friend, too.

I lean back against the wall behind me, the sauna's hot, dry air caressing my bare breasts, my stomach and thighs. Sweat trickles in rivulets all over my body and my clit throbs a little bit against its ring. Why can't any of this be simple?

"I hope he's cute at least," I say, letting my eyes fall closed and a fantasy begins to form in my mind. "Do you think he'll be handsome?"

Then the sauna door opens, and a girl around my age wafts in along with a gust of cool air. For a moment I'm too busy looking at her jewelry to really see her—taking in the diamonds that adorn her fingers and encircle her wrist, and the emeralds glittering darkly in her ears. Even barefaced in a towel, her hair swept back into a loose bun, she looks put together.

Then, once I can see past the glare of her jewels and the whiteness of her smile, I recognize her. It's been a few years, but Susan and I went to school together, at the same tiny, sheltered institution where families like ours send their daughters to prepare us for our true roles in life: as wives to powerful men, the glue that holds alliances—the business deals that come from them—together. She's slightly older than I am, which means that just about a year ago I was in Monaco, watching her walk down the aisle wearing a dress made of layers and layers of lace so sheer it looked like butterfly wings. The groom was a movie mogul, handsome and sharply put together, beaming at her in his jet-black tux.

She recognizes me, too. "Juliette!" she exclaims, slipping off her towel. "So funny running into you here!" We kiss each cheek, un-self-consciously naked.

"I know, what a nice coincidence."

Susan and Jane have met, just as I've met her companion Ingrid, many times. They greet each other with a wave, cognizant of the distance in their stations.

She takes a seat across from me, and I see why she looks so especially radiant: the towel was hiding a baby bump, her belly just starting to swell with the unmistakable sign that she's pregnant.

"Congratulations," I say, and she flushes slightly as she nods in quiet satisfaction. "When are you due?"

"February. It's a boy. We're naming him Theodore after my father in-law. Theodore Breckenridge the Fourth."

I'm seething with envy and having a really hard time hiding it.

"So," she says stretching her body in her seat. "I hear you're next down the aisle."

My cheeks are already pink from having been in the sauna, and I'm glad that she can't see that I'm startled by her words. "You heard that?" I ask.

"Everyone knows." She winks at me. "Where's your ring?"

It's so strange to think that other people know just as much about my engagement as I do. "Getting sized," I lie.

Susan shakes her head. "I suppose I'll see it at the wedding," she says. "Have you set a date?"

I hated the reminder that the date was contingent on my lessons. Why couldn't I just press fast-forward on life? "Not yet, but soon. You have to tell me about you, then— how is married life treating you? Is it like Christmas every day?"

Susan touches the ring on her left finger, with the biggest diamond of them all, almost unconsciously. "I'm so lucky," she says. "It's really been a dream. My husband takes such good care of me, I almost can't believe it. I worried, before, that I might be...a little bit bored. Or something. You just never know. But he takes me with him everywhere he goes, and the entire world is different with him beside me. We're just back from a week in Budapest, actually. Have you been to the Sziget Festival?"

"No." My father's interests are more traditional. The annual music festival is way too artistic and risqué for one of our trips. I find myself hoping that my husband is the arty type.

"Well, really I've been to so many music and art festivals I could use a break."

"Which was your favorite?"

As hotly envious as I am, I want to hear more. Any detail

could be fodder for a fantasy that will keep me going until I meet him.

"Shockingly? South by Southwest. It was so crowded, but we bought a house right in the middle of it all just to do the festival, and I swear, my husband did everything to make it feel like a home. He had his assistant buy a truckload of fresh flowers every day to make sure our house was always in bloom."

"He sounds really thoughtful," Jane says.

"He is. And generous." She flashes her ring and bracelet. "Obviously. And I surprise him with extraordinarily naughty lingerie." She touches her belly. Susan's laugh is sweet and easy; she sounds as joyful as I feel twisted up and confused. "He's my match," she says simply. "He understands how I was raised, and what I can do for him. I give him all of myself, and he gives me everything I need. I can't imagine my life any other way." She frowns slightly. "Well, I guess I can, but I don't want to."

I have to find some way to ask Susan about what's going on with Master and Palmer, without giving away what's going on with me, in case she's horrified. "Did he..." I start, trying to find the words to get at what I'm wondering about without revealing too much. "...was he your first?"

Susan looks confused. "Of course!" she says. "My goodness, who'd want a used wife?"

There's a displeased twist to her mouth, and suddenly I'm terrified that she thinks I was asking because I'd heard something about her, or worse, just assumed it. I have to backpedal, so I say, "Of course! I know! I just... I heard a story recently. About a girl who—you know—who's like us. And her husband made her go to some kind of sex school, where she got...she slept with another man before she'd even met him. So that she could learn how, or something."

Susan looks like I just told her that I knew a girl who

could make her head spin around 360 degrees; horrified and uncertain and definitely, definitely not like she's about to assure me that my little secret is perfectly normal and required of everyone. She shakes her head as she says, "That's weird. Too weird. It can't be true, don't you think?"

I nod furiously, carefully keeping my gaze on Susan so I don't have to see what Jane thinks of this exchange. I squeeze my legs a little bit tighter together, too, so that Susan won't catch a glimpse of the clit ring looped through my hood glinting, and start to wonder if the "friend" in my story might not actually be me.

"Absolutely," I say. "When I heard it, that's exactly what I thought. I was just seeing if you'd heard any rumors too."

SO I FEEL EVEN WORSE by the time Jane and I get to our massages. We're lying faceup on crisp Egyptian cotton, cucumbers on our eyes, while a man with hands that feel as strong as Master's look kneads the knots tied in my feet and calves.

"I'm going to refuse to go tomorrow," I tell Jane.

She doesn't usually disagree with me, so I'm surprised when she says, "I think you should go, Juliette. Really. He's not like any of the other matches, and once he marries you...think about it this way: this whole experience will be like a private secret you share."

I start to shake my head before realizing that I can't move without dislodging the cucumber. "I want to only think of him when I have sex. Not anyone else."

"What do you think it'll be like with him?" Jane asks. "Your husband?

The masseuse nudges my legs a little further apart so that he can start working on my thighs, and I have to concentrate not to shiver at the brush of his fingers against the inside of my leg, especially when I imagine my wedding night. Normally I wouldn't speak like this in front of a strange man, but the staff at Les Bains is highly discreet, and I'm certain they've heard worse than a schoolgirl fantasy or two.

"I don't know," I say. "But I hope it will be beautiful. I imagine our first time in our bed together. I would go back to Teresa's for lingerie—something a little bit demure, so that he can unwrap me like a present." When I was twelve we spent a week on an island off the coast of Italy, in a house that always smelled like ocean air and orange blossoms, and that's what I'm imagining now: silk sheets kissed with sun, my husband's hands sliding under the lace of my panties, his thumb parting my folds, finding my clit ring and giving it a gentle tug. The masseuse is still working steadily on my legs, stroking and kneading the muscle, and it's hard not to get that contact confused with the fantasy I'm spinning out for Jane.

"He would have roses all around the bedroom," I continue. "So many, the smell would seep into the drapes. The bed would be covered in petals. We'd have a glass of champagne together, to toast to our future. And then...he'd touch me. Anywhere he wanted, and all over. Because we both know that I'm his, and only his."

"Oh," Jane says, and I wonder if she's as turned on as I am right now, imagining a man's hands all over her body as her masseuse's glide across her skin. She clears her throat a little bit before she says, "I didn't...you've never really talked about the romance of it before. It's always sounded more like a business arrangement to me, I think."

I try to come up with a response to that, but my masseuse has started working on my outer hips, tugging my towel up so that it pools between my legs and leaves most of me exposed. His hands are so close to where I want them, and

I'm wet and throbbing between my legs; I can almost hear Antoine commanding me to spread, and I ache to follow his instructions, to let my body ask for what it wants.

Instead, all of a sudden, the masseuse's touch disappears. "All done," his soft, deep voice intones, and Jane and I both lie still and quiet as the two men leave the room.

"Have you imagined your wedding night?" I ask Jane.

"Oh," she says. "Yes. Of course. It's a little different than yours is, though."

"Tell me about it." Maybe Jane's fantasies will make the reality of my erotic finishing, and what's waiting for me at Jackson Palmer's tomorrow, feel a little less outrageous.

"I keep thinking about when Bruce fucked me with that screwdriver head," she says. "I was dying, I wanted him so badly, but the hottest part was when he just left me there with the tool inside of me, wondering who was going to walk in and see me. How they would know that I was a slut for him. And Juliette, I—" She pauses, as if to gather her courage, and then says, "I would have let them. I would have just stayed there, ass in the air, half naked, as long as he told me to. So that's what I want on my wedding night. Not the screwdriver, but the idea of him watching me touch myself—making me wait—God." Her voice is ragged with desire. "I want to be an exhibition. I want him to put me on display like I'm on a pedestal at the Met. I'd be his doll. His toy."

Then there's a sound like she's wriggling a little bit, trying to get comfortable under her towel, and I'm squirming, too. That is different, and sort of crazy, but it's also super hot. I loved it when Master had a room full of men watch me do ballet naked, and when Antoine painted me and put me on display as a piece of art; I can only imagine what it would feel like to have my husband's eyes on me as he commanded me to be filthy and depraved, and I obeyed with a helpless little moan.

I never would have guessed that was what Jane fantasized about; we've known each other forever, and its sort of delightful to learn something new about her. I like that we get to share this part of ourselves with each other—that she doesn't make me feel ashamed of the things I want, even if no one else in my life would understand them, or approve.

"I hope your dream happens for you," I say. "All of that and more."

"I hope the same for you," she says.

3

I FELT BETTER by the time I left the spa, but the next morning, as I'm sitting alone in the back of my town car being driven to Jackson Palmer's, I'm nervous again. Like Antoine, he lives on the coast, but in a ritzier part of town—newer money, flashier houses. Everything seems oversized and under-whelming, like the owners thought they could use the sheer size of their property to distract from their lack of taste. It makes me wonder who Jackson Palmer is and what he'll be like, and I'm glad to be distracted from my anxious vigil by my phone dinging with an incoming text.

It's from Daddy, an invitation to dinner at the big house tonight. Does he want to check in on how training is going? He'll be pleased to hear I haven't failed out yet, I suppose, though I also think he'd be furious if he knew where Rowan was taking me right now. The agency must have cleared all of this with my father, surely? Or maybe since it's what my husband wants, he doesn't matter. Even if what my husband wants still confuses me.

Anyway, he needs an answer about dinner. *As long as*

Talia's not making something with mushrooms again, I write back.

We turn off the main road, then, and go up a small hill to where a big white house that looks just like the rest of them is perched. The roof and the tiling in the courtyard are both terra-cotta; the tinkling of water falling into a deep blue fountain is the only sound other than the wind. It looks like the Mediterranean as built by someone who'd only ever heard about it; the place manages to feel both luxurious but also curiously impersonal. Like if a therapist designed a hotel. I can't imagine losing my virginity to a stranger at all, but I definitely don't want to do it *here*.

Rowan turns the car off and settles in to wait while I walk up to the door and ring the bell. Then there's a long pause while I wait for someone to answer.

Why is it always like this, I wonder? What is it with these men and making me wait?

For once, though, I don't mind, since I already know I'm not looking forward to this lesson. I'm still trying to figure out how I can negotiate myself some kind of deal with Mr. Palmer, Sex Practitioner, that doesn't involve penetration. At this point, my blow job skills are first rate—maybe that'll net me an early graduation?

When Jackson finally does open the door, he's handsome —movie star-handsome, with a caramel tan and white teeth and piercing blue eyes that feel designed to throw me off-balance. He's wearing linen pants and a summer sweater, a light, airy outfit that matches the beachy, light-filled interior of his house.

"Juliette," he says, taking one of my hands between his. "So good to meet you."

I summon up all of the politeness that's been trained into me since childhood. I will *not* just burst out with "I don't want to fuck you" first thing, especially because, under other circumstances, I absolutely would—he's gorgeous, and something about the way he holds himself reminds me of Master, a sense of intense, restrained self-possession that always makes me wet. It's not Jackson himself I have a problem with. It's our circumstances.

"Nice to meet you as well," I say.

He ushers me in, and I follow him through the foyer to a palatial living room. "Was the drive all right?" he asks.

"Just fine," I assure him.

"I'm glad," he says. "Traffic can be a buzzkill, and that's something this neighborhood likes to do by itself."

That coaxes a smile out of me; I like that he can joke about this place, that he seems to understand that where he lives is beautiful, but also a little ridiculous.

"Do you need anything?" he asks. "Water? We have sparkling or still. Some clients like to have a glass of wine or champagne, though of course I hope you'll feel comfortable either way."

"I'd love a glass of wine, please," I hear myself say. I had planned on trying to be careful with him, making sure he knew that I wasn't going to be a pushover, but he's good at his job—even after just a few minutes, I'm more relaxed than I thought I would be. I realize I had been expecting someone a little more…intense, maybe, who would approach me the way Vlad and Antoine did, who would want his fingers in my pussy before he'd bothered to learn my name. Jackson, in contrast, feels warm and personable, as if he's someone I could actually enjoy spending time with.

I don't know what to do with that.

"Red or white?" he asks.

"White," I say. This feels like the wrong place to end up with a wine-stained tongue.

He gestures for me to take a seat in the living room and then leaves to get me my drink, which gives me an opportunity to look around. The house is sparsely decorated—all of the furniture is white and stark, and there's not a single personal object or memento, not even a photograph. As charming as Jackson is in real life, he doesn't seem to have left a trace of that personality on this space.

The view is gorgeous, though: two of the windows overlook the beach, and I'm watching the waves crash, cerulean and spume, against the shore when he returns. He hands me the glass and then settles himself on a couch across from me.

"I fell in love with this Sancerre in France last year," he says. "It's so crisp and fresh; it always reminds me of the first days of spring, when winter has just thawed and those first green buds are poking their heads up. That felt right for our first session together."

I take a sip and let the flavors wash over my palate. I tend to prefer something heartier, but he's right that this is lovely, an easy balance of mineral and floral that briefly distracts me from what we're here to do.

Then Jackson puts his glass down and says, "So, Juliette. Tell me about yourself."

I mirror him and put my own glass down, then clear my throat and sit back.

"I'm twenty-one," I tell him. "I've been privately tutored with other girls in my circle since I was five or so, and I've always done really well in whatever I tried. Dressage. Calculus. Ballet." I think of my most recent ballet lessons, which took place with my instructor's hands between my legs more often than not, and flush. "My father is William Newmont," I say, pausing to see if he'll recognize the name or not. I'm never sure how much these tutors understand my world, whether they're truly part of it, or just exist in service of it. "He works as a—"

"That's fine," Jackson says. "I don't want you thinking about your father right now." His smile is so contagious that I find myself smiling back at him as he says, "What was your favorite thing you learned in all these lessons?"

The answer is at the tip of my tongue, because of course I have a favorite thing. Physics. Greek. Data analysis. But three full seconds later, I haven't answered, because nothing stands out. Nothing. It's all the same. I learned it. I excelled. I moved on. "I loved all of it the same," I say without a trace of a lie.

"When did you first start masturbating?"

It catches me off guard, but at least it's a question with a definite answer.

"When I was a teenager," I tell him. "I don't remember exactly when. Fourteen, I guess?"

He nods. "Have you ever used toys on yourself?"

"Not for penetration." I've seen them, of course, in some of the kinkier lingerie shops I've visited, but I've never bought one for myself. I didn't want to mess with my hymen in case my husband was particular about that kind of thing, and anyway, I assumed I'd learn all about toys in bed with him after we married...if he wanted me to.

Jackson's voice drops just slightly and I shiver as he asks me, "When you touch yourself, what do you fantasize about?"

Oh. Um.

I can't tell him the truth, which is that it used to be a variety of men—movie stars, or some of my father's handsomer business associates; the waiter who snuck me extra champagne at an endless dinner in Geneva and a man I saw at a ski lodge in the Alps one winter, stripping out of his ski pants, ruddy and breathless after a day on the slopes. Recently, though, when I think of them I feel empty, disinterested, and it's only when I picture Master—his eyes and face, his hands, his long, thick cock, that my body hums with want.

"Men," I say to start with, because that's safe and obvious enough. "I think about...about what sex with a man would be like." Especially if he had green eyes and a wicked smile. "What it would feel like to be touched by him." If he put me over his knee and spanked me again, but this time, after, he slipped his fingers between my legs and fucked me with them until I came for him once, and then again.

"Can you be more specific?" Jackson asks. "When you picture your first time, for instance?"

"Sure. Uh, I mean, I imagine a bed," I say. "Of rose petals." I try to remember what I was telling Jane yesterday, when the masseuse was right between my thighs and I was too turned on to censor myself. "The room would have flowers everywhere." Susan's trip to Budapest and my own fantasies are getting mixed up. "Roses," I correct myself. "We'd drink champagne." It all should sound very romantic, but now the words fall flat, and I wonder if Jackson's going to laugh at my little-girl ideas about what sex is like.

"When you say 'we,'" Jackson says. "Are you imagining anyone specific?"

"Nope." If I can't even tell him about how I've fantasized about losing my virginity, I definitely can't tell him about how I think of Master. I'm not ready to expose that part of myself yet. Master wasn't even supposed to be in a car alone with me, apparently; what if my feelings get him in trouble?

But also, I don't want him to be part of a game we're playing here. He's not something Jackson should use to get off either of us. What happens in my head with Master is private, and I want it to stay that way.

"Not an actor, or musician?" Jackson prompts. "Maybe an athlete?"

I shrug helplessly. "Nope," I repeat. "I don't like to be too specific. Just a generic handsome guy."

This is the first time in this interaction that Jackson's been displeased with me; it feels like the sun disappearing behind the clouds. "Do you understand what we're going to do here?" he asks. "What you're going to learn?"

Okay. It's time. *Be brave, Juliette.* I say, "I wanted to talk to you about that."

Jackson waits.

"It's just that... my virginity. That's something that's important to me, and I think it will be important to my husband, too. Or it should be. I don't want to question your methods and I don't want to cause trouble, but I have to ask —is there any way I can do the training and stay a virgin?"

"You've never been touched sexually?"

"I have."

"Have you had oral sex?"

"Yes."

"So, you don't want to break your hymen?"

"Yes. Is that possible at all?"

Jackson nods thoughtfully, and considers my request for a long time before he answers. I sip my wine and count the waves breaking on shore: one, two, three, four, five, six, before he says, "We can certainly start without any penetration, but I can't make any promises without a discussion with your master. Let's get started, then decide where to go from there, okay?"

I assumed he was going to flat-out deny my request; I wouldn't have been surprised if he'd insisted on fucking me on this couch right now, and I would have done it, too. I'm so relieved that I know he can see it on my body, and I'm glad— it's a better thanks than anything I could say out loud.

"Follow me," he says, standing up. I trail him to another, smaller room, this one without quite so many windows, though it's still just as enormous and airy, in part because one of the walls is covered in floor-to-ceiling mirrors that remind me of the dance studio. There's also a large bed fitted with navy sheets; it's one of the first non-white things I've seen in the house, and I like the way it anchors the room, makes it feel a little more traditional and masculine. I wonder if this is where Jackson fucks all of his clients. I wonder if he sleeps here, too, or if he has his own bedroom somewhere else in the house.

"Would you feel comfortable taking off your clothes?" Jackson asks, distracting me from my curiosity. His voice already feels like a caress against my skin, and I imagine it would feel even better, warmer and more intimate, if I was naked. "There's a robe there you can wear if you want."

I nod, and he looks away respectfully while I slip my dress over my head and step out of my heels before peeling off my bra and panties. It's so different than any of my experiences with my tutors so far, and I revel in the feeling of safety as I wrap myself in the robe he's provided.

"Ready?" he asks.

"Ready."

"Okay. Take a seat, please." He indicates a small padded stool that's been placed in front of the floor-to-ceiling mirror.

I follow instructions, looking shyly at my reflection as I take my seat. My hair is loose around my shoulders, and my face looks different than I've ever seen it before—I look shy but also happy, pleasure starting to glow in my cheeks.

"I'm going to get between your legs now, Juliette," Jackson says. "Open them for me?"

I do, swallowing a moan at the feeling of exposing myself, my bare pussy, already wet from being in a room with this gorgeous man, now open for him to see.

"Can I open your robe, too?"

I'm breathless, almost dizzy with want, so I just nod. He unties the belt and slips it open, so that he can see my cunt, my breasts, my belly. I've been naked in rooms with dozens of men, at this point, but I don't know that I've ever felt as seen as I do when Jackson's eyes skate down my skin, drinking me in like he wants to swallow me whole.

"Look at you," he breathes. "Gorgeous, Juliette. I love how responsive your body is, the way your nipples are already hard for me. I like it when my partners are turned on." His smile is still soft, but there's something dirty in it now, too, that makes my stomach go tight with need.

"If you wanted me to, I'd put my mouth on them while I touched you. I love feeling the way a woman clutches around my fingers. There's nothing in the world like the heat inside of a pussy. It's velvet. It drives me crazy."

No one's ever talked to me like this—described my body with words I mostly only hear in my head. It's so hot to see this man, who ten minutes ago I thought was sweet and polite, talking about how badly he wants to get his tongue inside of me, to let me suck his cock while I play with myself.

"First, though," he says, "we should make sure you're familiar with your body. What it is, and what it does." He smooths a hand over my mound and says, "This is your pubis, and then here," he presses lightly with the heel of his hand, "is your clit. That's your pleasure center, Juliette. Do you like having the hood pierced?"

"I do."

"Good. Good. Below that are your labia—these lips here." He drags his fingers along my folds, and I know he can feel how wet I am for him. I lift my hips, beckoning him to where I'm dripping.

"Slow down," he says, taking his time as he runs his hand down my slit. "We're still learning anatomy."

I already know the names of my erotic organs, thank you very much, and if he wants me to beg in clinical terms I can certainly say *I need your phalanges in my vagina ASAFP.*

I'm trying my best to remember patience, but once again my hips buck, urging him lower.

"Perhaps you'll be less eager if you're in charge," he says, walking behind me and to the side so he's out of the picture. "Put your fingers inside yourself, Juliette."

I do as he asks and feel the immediate relief of penetration.

"That's your vulva," he says. "And it's got muscles you can use to give yourself and your partner pleasure. Can you try to flex them a little bit? Clamp down on your finger, and imagine it's someone's cock, buried deep in your pussy."

It takes a second to coordinate, but I do it, and it feels so good that I let out a small moan of pleasure.

"Yes," he says. "Yes, just like that. That's called a Kegel. You can keep going with them if you like. I'd like to see you come for me, Juliette."

I start to fuck myself onto my fingers, tightening around them in rhythm as the pressure at the base of my spine builds and builds. Any tension that I felt previously melts away, and I love knowing that Jackson is watching me, that he can see my hips starting to rock as I get closer and closer, chasing the friction that will push me over the edge. I imagine the things he talked about—his mouth on my pussy, and then his cock pushing inside of me—and come with a cry, muscles pulsing as I shake through my orgasm.

When I look up, Jackson is smiling at me. "Lovely," he says. "Your homework tonight is to go home and try that again. Touch yourself as much as you can, and figure out exactly what you like."

I'm relieved I've gotten through this unscathed, but then he says, "Tomorrow, it likely won't be fingers inside you."

4

Before I can do my homework, I have to go to dinner with my father. It's unusual for him to have me up to the big house, especially these days—I typically eat in the guest cottage where I live, which is fine with me. Dressing for dinner with Daddy is a whole to-do, and most days, I'm happy to avoid it in favor of a more casual meal at my kitchen table.

This particular evening, though, I slip on a silvery sheath dress and a pair of open-toed sandals to show off my brand-new pedicure; my feet are finally recovering from the beating they took during ballet lessons with Vlad, and I'm extremely grateful. Our butler, Damon, nods politely as he holds the front door open and informs me that my father is waiting for me in the sitting room.

Daddy greets me with cheek kisses and a glass of wine. I'm glad to have something to do with my hands; lately, being here always makes me slightly nervous, which makes sense. Last time we had dinner together, it was because I was about to fail out of the program all together, and he was livid with me. I take a quick glance around the sitting room, but everything is exactly as it usually is, so there's no hint as to why I'm here except for a pale pink bakery box sitting on one of the side tables.

It's from LonnyCakes. My favorite.

My father seems to be in a good mood as he settles into the leather and teak armchair by the fireplace. "How's that new round of training going?" he asks.

How can I possibly answer that? *Today Jackson Palmer, professional sex expert, told me he wanted to eat my cunt and taught me how to come on my own fingers?* "Not so bad, really," I tell him. "All good. I'm fine."

"Fine? This isn't calculus, dear."

I sip my wine and raise my eyebrows at him over the rim of the glass. He knows what I'm doing, surely? He was the one who first told me that I'd be required to participate in some erotic finishing, after all. "I'm learning a lot, and it's not calculus," I say.

Daddy shakes his head. "Say no more. I'm not supposed to ask details because frankly, I don't want them."

I don't blame him.

"All I need to know is that you feel safe and taken care of," he continues.

Safe and taken care of. Is that how I feel? I've asked myself a lot of questions throughout this training period—*why am I doing this, should I quit, is any man worth all of this*—but never that one before.

Maybe that's because I didn't have to. Because when I do think about it, I find that, to my surprise, that the answer is yes. I've done so many things I never thought I'd do—posing nude, allowing someone to pierce one of the most intimate parts of my body, getting on my knees and sucking cock for a man who wasn't my husband. But none of that felt dangerous. And I certainly never felt like I couldn't stop what was happening if I decided I needed to.

Which, of course, is because of Master. He's brusque and arrogant; he can be stony and unfeeling, and he's driven me crazy just as often as he's turned me on. But I've always known that he was in charge, and that he wouldn't let anyone hurt me. I remember him distracting me before Antoine stuck the needle through my clit hood, and the way he wiped my tears away after, and I know that, even if he's vowed never to let me into his car or his life again, he doesn't want to see me suffer. That promise is as iron-clad as his self-control. I don't know if I could do this without him, but as long as he sticks around, I'm okay.

"I am safe and taken care of," I say to Daddy, "and I'm not telling you anything else."

He seems satisfied with that answer. "Good," he says. "A business partner is coming for dinner. Do you remember Vaughn Devonshire?"

Daddy has dozens of partners across the world; I've met them periodically at parties and whatnot over the years, especially once my mother wasn't around to attend functions with him. I've been trained to remember faces and names flawlessly—it's a skill I'll need as the wife of a man with international business connections, so that I can extend invitations and write thank-you notes, as well as socialize on behalf of our family. But this name doesn't call anyone to mind, which means I must have met him before I got good at it.

"Vaughn Devonshire?" I repeat to see if that jogs a memory. "Probably." Now that I feel more confident that I'm not in trouble, I get up and walk around the room a little bit. I always get restless after one of my lessons, even if this one involved less sitting around than Antoine's did. I go over to the bakery box and lift the lid. Inside is a beautiful little cake, its smooth vanilla frosting dotted with candied violets. "Oooh, lavender buttercream! This for tonight?"

"Yes. Vaughn has a keen interest in French Romanticism," Daddy says. "He doesn't get to talk about it much. I thought you'd have a lot to—" Daddy slaps my hands away before I can complete my mission of swiping a violet. "Get your fingers out of there. You can have some after dinner."

"Um, no," I say. "I'm not interested in sitting through dinner to get Stendhal mansplained to me. But maybe I'll come back for cake?"

He shrugs. "Go amuse yourself," he says. "We'll call you for the buttercream."

———

THE THING IS, I don't really *want* to do my homework. There were days when I was dying to touch myself, mostly when Master told me I couldn't, but now that it's been assigned, it seems less amusing and more like…well. Work. So I knock on Jane's door to see if she's around to distract me.

She isn't.

Maybe I can just skip my homework, then? It's not like there's a worksheet I have to bring in, or a test that's coming up. And it's not like I've never masturbated before. I can make something up in the morning.

It's been a long day, so I leave my bedroom door ajar and slip into the bathroom to take a long, hot, luxurious bath. I turn on the taps and watch water rush into the tub's slick porcelain belly; I throw in a rose-scented bath bomb that turns the water pink and decorates it with fragments of dried petals.

I ease myself into the water and lean my head back, letting my eyes fall closed. After months of tutoring, trying hard even when I don't know what I'm doing, it feels like an intense luxury to just float for a while—let go of asking my body to do anything, and let it be for a while.

The feel of the water and the scent of the roses reminds me of the spa, though, of the fantasies I shared with Jane. Alone in this quiet room it feels safe to admit to myself what I really want: Master doing all of those things with me, pouring me champagne and decorating a room in rose petals, sliding his hands under my robe. I try to distract myself—imagine what china pattern I'll pick out for my wedding, who will design my dress, where we'll go on our first vacation, but as always, Master's presence intrudes, and I imagine myself doing each one of those things with him, instead of my actual husband.

By the time the water starts to cool off and I'm ready to get out, I'm already more than a little turned on, and I decide that I may as well at least try to do my homework, since I'm already naked and everything.

I sit in front of my mirror, legs spread, and try again to refocus my mind on myself and my husband, but it doesn't work. Last time I saw myself like this, in this particular glass, I was riding Master's suit-clad thigh to orgasm. I slip my fingers inside of myself the way Jackson taught me to and flex around them, trying to think of Antoine, Vlad, the men who saw me in that art show and the ones who watched me dance naked in the ballet studio. The singer I used to crush on when I was still just a kid fumbling around in bed at night. Anyone but Master.

Every time I succeed, though, something happens—there's a faint, masculine scent drifting in from somewhere, and it reminds me of him so much that I can't concentrate. I Kegel on my fingers and every time I close my eyes it's just Master feeding his cock down my throat, Master with his hands between my legs, Master cupping my breasts and thumbing at my nipples, his mouth hot and wet against my neck. I'm about to give up and come for him, let the fantasy of him push me over the edge, when I hear a man clear his throat.

I leap up and grab a towel, wrapping it around myself as quickly as I can. "Who's there?"

A man peers around the half-open door—I left it that way so that Jane would come find me when she got home, but this is definitely not Jane. He's older, in his late 30's, maybe, with the beginnings of salt-and-pepper streaking through his dark hair. His jaw is strong and his curly hair is tousled, and the sight of him, so close to the orgasm I didn't have, almost takes my breath away.

"My name's Vaughn Devonshire," he says.

I'm too undone to keep my mouth shut. "French Romantics, Vaughn?" I blurt.

"Indeed." He holds my gaze shamelessly, and my skin prickles with want. I'm pretty sure he just saw what I was doing, and even if he didn't, he doesn't pretend modesty— though he also doesn't ogle me openly. The way he looks at me is frank, and interested. And hot. "Your father said you weren't hungry," he says.

Not for food, but that's none of his business. "Okay…"

"But you were interested in dessert?" he finishes.

"And he couldn't just text me?" I'm not sure I trust Vaughn.

But "He did, apparently," Vaughn says, and I remember that of course, I left my phone in my bedroom, so that it wouldn't bother me while I was relaxing.

"The door was open, but I should have knocked," Vaughn says. His words are apologetic but as he says them, his gaze drops, and I can almost feel it brushing my shoulders, my collarbone, the tops of my breasts and my bare legs, still dripping with bathwater, as it goes.

"It's okay," I say.

"If you ever want to discuss the French…" And just like

that, he's looking at me again, shameless, fire-eyed and wanting. We both know exactly what he means, and I think that maybe I could come like this, just with his eyes on me, that gaze as silky and firm as any lover's caress.

"I'll let you know," I say, and I'm surprised by how husky my voice sounds. I clear my throat. I have to get this situation under control.

"Good." Vaughn smiles at me, and his smirk makes me hot all over. "I'm going to head back for dessert," he says, and then he turns and leaves.

When I glance back in the mirror, I'm as pink as my bathwater, blushing from toes to cheeks.

5

ON THE RIDE to Jackson's in the morning, pale yellow sunlight drifts through the car windows, sweet and clear, but I'm feeling unsettled. After Vaughn left last night, I got dressed again and went up to the big house, only to find that he wasn't there. I ate cake with Daddy, and even though I'd gone out of my way to avoid seeing Vaughn at dinner, assuming he'd bore me to sleep, I couldn't help being disappointed. I went to bed early, and only realized when I woke up this morning that not only had I not been able to actually talk to Vaughn... I didn't finish my homework, either.

So I'm feeling a little blue when Jackson opens the door and leads me to the living room, with its enormous picture windows looking onto another beautiful day.

"How did your homework go?" he asks when we're seated. He's just as handsome as he was yesterday, and I feel guilty for letting him down.

"Fine," I tell him.

"Fine?"

"I didn't get to finish," I explain. Maybe honesty will win

me points here. "I was…interrupted. By one of my dad's business partners."

Jackson nods slowly. "Tell me about that," he says. "Describe it for me."

"I took a bath," I say. The memory makes me flush with desire and shame, made all the hotter by the fact of having Jackson's eyes on me, his gaze as tempting and titillating as Vaughn's was last night. "I used a bath bomb, and the room smelled like rose petals, and it reminded me…it reminded me of a fantasy I've had. So when I got out, I looked at myself in the mirror, and touched myself, like we practiced."

"Did it feel good, or were you just doing it because that's what I'd told you to do?"

"Both," I say, my stomach twisting as I admit it to him. "I liked the idea that I was pleasing you. And I liked the way it felt to have my fingers inside of me."

"What were you thinking about while you did it?"

"I was thinking about what I looked like," I say. "Because I was looking in the mirror. About how I would look if anyone saw me. With my legs spread like that, and my fingers in my pussy. They would know how badly I want it."

"And then someone did see you, didn't they?"

"They did. He did."

"Did you like it?"

"I was embarrassed," I say.

Jackson waits, like he knows that's not all.

"But it was hot, too. The thought of just letting someone see me like that. Doing something so secret and private in public. I don't know. It made everything more intense."

"What happened? When he interrupted you?"

"I was close," I say, closing my eyes. It all comes rushing back to me: the tension building in my muscles as I flexed on my fingers, the tightness in my belly and the sense that it was all about to spiral out into an orgasm. The sound of Vaughn's voice and the smell of his cologne. "He—I think he'd been watching for a while, but that's when he said something. I— as soon as I knew he was there, I put on a towel, and we talked a little bit. My dad had sent him down to get me. They had had dinner together, and I didn't want to join, but there was going to be cake for dessert, from LonnyCakes, and I had said I wanted a piece, so." I shrug, twisting my fingers in the hem of my skirt. The story is a bit of a dud at the end. "I did go up and get some cake after, but he was gone by then, so. That's it."

Jackson surprises me by asking, "How was the cake?"

I want to shoot back with a *why do you care?* Instead, I laugh.

"Anti-climactic," I say. "I was excited about it because it had lavender buttercream frosting, and that flavor is the one I always choose for special occasions. Normally it's the best thing I've ever tasted." I shrug. "Last night's was meh, though. Maybe they changed the recipe."

Jackson nods thoughtfully, like there's something to what I just said, instead of a description of an aborted orgasm and a mediocre cake. Whatever it is, though, he doesn't tell me about it. He just stands up and says, "Are you ready to begin, Juliette?"

I nod.

"Take your clothes off, and get on the couch."

There's that tone again: gentle but still commanding, kind but also unquestionably firm. It feels like the stroke that precedes a slap, and I love the sensation of his voice in my mind and on my skin.

We're still in the room with all the windows; yesterday, he brought me into a more private space before he asked me to undress. We're up too high for anyone to see, but still, I can't help wondering if anyone on the beach might look up and notice, and it makes me feel the same excitement and shame that pricked me last night. I think of Vaughn's eyes on me as I unbutton the dress I wore and let it slide off my shoulders. I step out of my panties and unhook my bra, saving my heels for last. Then, when I'm completely naked, I sit down on the couch.

Jackson kneels in front of me. "Open your legs," he says.

I do it in a daze. Seeing him like this in front of me, all of his power and charm contained between my spread knees, is already a lot to take in. Not to mention the muscles of his chest and shoulders, coiled and thick under his smooth, tan skin.

He says, "Has anyone ever eaten you out before?"

I shake my head *no*.

He doesn't say anything else, just leans forward and presses his tongue against my clit, closing his mouth around it to give it a little suck.

"Oh," I hear myself say. "Oh, oh, oh my God."

Jackson doesn't respond; he uses his hands to press my thighs apart and keeps licking me open, pausing occasionally to tug on my clit ring with his teeth.

I lean back on my hands so I can tilt my hips forward just a tiny bit, chasing the sensation of him against me, wet where I'm wet, soft where I'm soft. I've never felt anything as filthy and delicious as his mouth against my pussy, tongue lapping hungrily at my entrance. My breathing is coming faster, in little startled spurts, like I keep forgetting how my lungs work.

When he moves a hand down and presses a finger inside of me, there's no resistance; my body is grateful for the pressure and fullness he provides.

"Let me feel you," he murmurs, so I squeeze around him. He curls his finger, stroking against the roof of my pussy, and licks my clit again, coaxing me helplessly towards my orgasm. I can't stop picturing what I'll look like to anyone who can see in through those windows: riding this man's face, taking my pleasure, coming for him on his fingers and his tongue.

But what would they think if I was riding his cock? If they could see how greedy I was for more. If Master could see.

"Wait—" I start, the fingers I have tangled in his hair now pulling him back.

"Is something wrong?" he asks.

Only that I'm feeling eager to get this over with. "I'm ready for it now."

He demands clarification. "Ready for…what?"

"Ready for your cock."

He smiles as though my answer pleases him, but I also sense it would have been okay if I wasn't ready for more. I understand why Master sent me here. Jackson's patience is reassuring. I am safe and cared for.

"Lie back," he says, and I do, following his command like I've been hypnotized. He stands up and undoes his fly. His cock is thicker than Antoine's was, but just as hard for me, red and flushed all over, wet at the tip.

He kneels back down again, standing up on his knees, this time, and presses the head of his cock against my entrance.

I wait, prepared for the moment that will change me. I think it's going to be easy. I think it's just going to happen. But instead, all of a sudden, I'm frozen. My body is locked down, resistant. He nudges himself against me, rubs my clit with his fingers, tries to get us back to where we were a few seconds ago, but the moment is gone, and I know it.

"I'm sorry," I say, staring up at the ceiling. "I don't know what's wrong with me."

"You're anxious. Close your eyes. Imagine the fantasies from last night."

I try. I imagine Vaughn feeding me buttercream. But

when he tries again, I'm just as unyielding. I don't understand.

I feel completely useless and humiliated, and this time, not in a hot way. "I just... I don't think I can."

"That's all right."

I expect him to walk away, then, frustrated with me and my uncooperative body, to call Master. Instead he slides back down between my legs and puts his mouth on me again. This time there's no playing around, no soft touches or exploratory, teasing licks; he holds my hips against his face with one hand and fucks me with his tongue, domineering and expert, until I understand that he is my master in this moment and then I'm coming for him, cunt spasming around nothing, orgasm ripping through me like wildfire.

I'm boneless by the time he stands up again, cock still hard, and says, "You should be nice and relaxed now. Just open up and let me fuck you, Juliette."

I want to. I want to so badly. I want to obey his command and I want to be good for him and I want that cock inside of me, but again, when he presses against me, I clamp shut.

Still, I can't give up. "Keep going," I urge him. "I'm sure—"

"No," he says. "This isn't something you need to get over with. It's something to enjoy. To savor." He stands over me, stroking himself, and I imagine what I must look like to him, panting and wrung out from the way he took me apart, but too selfish to give him his pleasure. "Can you imagine what it would be like to take my cock? How good it would feel to have something bigger than a couple of fingers inside of you?"

I close my eyes and try to picture it, but the image is strangely impersonal—like watching porn, not like one of my actual fantasies, which are almost too vivid sometimes. I'm still wet, and I think I might like to touch myself, but I just... I'm not sure how to want Jackson. I can't picture us having sex, not actually. Not in a way that makes me want it.

"You're scared," he says. "But there's nothing to be afraid of, really. You just had a lovely orgasm for me; now I want us to have one together. Imagine how it will feel, with your tight little pussy clenching me like that instead of your hands or your mouth. Imagine how I'll fill you up. How you'll milk all the pleasure from me when you come again and again, all over my cock."

I can imagine it. I can imagine every second of it. But somehow what I'm imagining feels distant, something for a more experienced Juliette to enjoy. It doesn't feel like my first time.

He comes a little closer. "Sit up," he says. "Look how simple it is." He fucks into his hand as he watches me, not bothering to hide his appreciation of my body as he touches himself. I watch his cock disappearing into the sheath of his fist over and over again and even though I know it would feel amazing buried inside of me, touching places no one else has touched, the image still leaves me oddly cold. He reaches out a hand to my shoulder and holds me in place while he spurts all over my tits, leaving me dripping with his cum.

"What did you think of that?" he asks.

"It was hot," I say, because it was. "But...it was like my mind was turned on, but my body couldn't get there. I've never felt this way before. I don't know what to do about it."

"Well," he says. "That's a problem we have to address. Your mind and your body have a broken connection. Wait here."

I sit on the couch, still stark naked, and suddenly aware of the damp spot underneath me where my own wetness and Jackson's spit pooled between my legs. Is someone going to have to clean this up later? What will they think of me, that I sat here and let someone I barely know eat me out, but couldn't figure out how to let him fuck me?

Jackson returns a few minutes later with a simple brown shopping bag that would look cheap except for the pink ribbon handles. "There's a gift for you in there," he says. "A dildo, so you can use that when you practice, instead of just your fingers. Go home tonight and fantasize about whatever you want—whatever makes you the hottest, the most on fire. Explore. Experiment. No rush, and no pressure, okay?"

He hands me the bag, and I peek into it. The dildo is probably a little smaller than Jackson's cock, but it's still sizeable enough that I know it's not going to work. "This is going to break it," I tell him.

"Break what?"

Why does no one understand this? "My hymen?" I remind him. "I won't be a virgin."

Jackson's smile is not unkind. "Juliette," he says. "That's the point."

6

WHEN I GET HOME that evening, I lock the guest house's front door behind me out of habit.

Then I unlock it. Just in case. To see what happens. If anyone comes in.

But no. I'm being silly. I lock it again.

Then I go to my bedroom and put a chair in front of my mirror. Put the dildo on my bedside table. I won't skimp on homework tonight. Jackson didn't seem *that* frustrated with me, but still, I don't want to test his patience. I want to be good at this. I don't understand what's wrong with me.

I try to set the mood for myself: I turn my overhead lights off, opting for the smaller sconces on the walls, and light a few candles. I take off my clothes again and spread my legs, trying to summon residual arousal from earlier. I palm my breasts, pinch my nipples, lick my index finger and circle it around my clit.

I may as well be brushing my teeth for all it does for me. There's no way the dildo is going to go in me like this. I'm starting to hate the whole exercise and also myself, which is definitely not how this is supposed to go. I can't fail this. I don't fail. But I also can't seem to succeed.

I fling myself down on my bed and, without letting myself think about it too much, I put my earbuds in and call Master.

He picks up with a curt "Yes?"

He's at a party or something—I can hear music in the background, and people talking and laughing. I try very hard not to be jealous.

"This isn't working," I tell him.

"It's eleven o'clock at night."

"This homework...it's..." I can't finish. If I tell him it's too hard or I'm not into it, he's not going to care.

His voice is crisp with impatience when he says, "What is it, Juliette?"

"It's just not working. I can't use the dildo. Just can't."

I was hoping to provoke him a little bit—his pity, maybe, or at least his interest. Instead, he sounds angry. "Palmer is there to help with this."

His irritation inflames something inside of me. His attention feels like the sun on my skin, even when he's mad, and I want more of it.

"I'm dry!" I cry out. "How am I supposed to do this if I can't get wet?"

I can almost hear his scowl through the phone. "You're calling me over a failure of imagination."

"My imagination's just fine!" It is, too. I set the mood. I followed instructions. I thought about a man's hands and a man's voice and a man's eyes on my skin. It's not my fault that none of that worked. Or if it is, I don't know how to fix it.

"Obviously, it's not fine."

I try another tactic. "Maybe if I knew who I was fantasizing about—"

"Stop!" The sudden intensity of his response resounds through my body, vibrating me like a plucked string. I hear the slap of a sliding door being closed, and then there's nothing but his breath on the line, the faint sounds of crickets and the breeze. "Your imagination solves that problem with a blindfold."

Oh, I think. *He's right.*

I close my eyes and imagine rough hands on my shoulders, tying a piece of black silk carefully around my head. I close my eyes and the darkness feels specific, instead of impersonal.

"I get it," I say. "But what does he sound like?"

The sound from his side gets muffled as if his hand is covering the microphone. He's talking, but I don't know what he's saying. Then the muffle is gone and I hear the last moments of a woman's laugh.

"You there?" he asks me.

"I'm sorry. I'll go."

"You can't." His voice is gravel and smoke. "You're tied to the headboard by the elbows and your knees are bent up and wide open. Your cunt is open for anyone to see."

I push myself backwards on the bed and arrange myself exactly like that, spreading for him, cunt pulsing as all the wetness I couldn't summon suddenly appears, immediately, at his command.

"What kind of slut are you?" he says with his mouth far from the phone.

"Your little slut."

"I wasn't talking to you, but good. Good. There's a man. You can't see him, but you feel him when he slaps your pussy." There's a slapping sound from his side, and a woman yips. "Hush," he says to her.

"He grabs your ass and spreads you apart. Rubs his thumb

on your asshole. Do it, Juliette. Rub your asshole." Away from the phone, he says, "Get on those pretty knees."

My finger circles my tight pucker, and it yields just a little. I've never felt anything like it.

"You wonder if he's going to fuck your ass, and you won't be able to do a thing about it. You're helpless." The way he says it makes me feel powerless and submissive. If Master tells me to put the dildo in my ass, I know I will.

"Then, he puts two fingers inside your cunt." With my other hand, I do what he says while he talks to the woman he's with. I envy her desperately when he whispers, "Take my cock out like a good little whore."

In my mind, I'm in both places. Blindfolded in a bedroom with a strange man fingering my asshole, and at a party with Master, on my knees, freeing his cock.

"He's going to fuck you," he says to me. Now, I can tell the difference in tone when he talks to me and when he talks to her. "He's going to do whatever he wants to you. You know you're safe because I say you are." He changes tone. "But this man is rough with you. Do you trust him?"

"Yes."

My answer is always *yes,* where Master is concerned. My pussy is sweet and slick now, and I toy with my clit ring, tugging on it the way that Jackson did when he was eating me out earlier. I rub the little circle against myself and a short cry falls out of my mouth.

"You ask who he is, but he just puts his fingers in your mouth to shut you up, and you suck them like a good little whore," Master says, and I know he's doing to her what he's saying to me, talking to both of us. "Now take my cock all the way down."

It's everything I can do to hang on at this point, to keep breathing as he takes me apart through the telephone line.

"Just relax, my dirty slut. I'm going to fuck that pretty mouth." I'm sucking on my own fingers now. Jealous of whoever he's with and so turned on by them together I can't think straight. "He slaps your body like meat," he says to me. "Your tits, your ass, your cunt." The woman on the other side gasps in surprise. I am her, and I gasp too.

"Your throat's so tight," he says breathing hard, there with me, slapping me everywhere, fingering my ass, fucking my mouth, pinching my clit. I'm on my knees on the patio while everyone's watching me suck his dick, and I'm on my bed with my legs in the air and two fingers inside me. "Take it all." He grunts to her, and I obey.

"He fucks you, hummingbird," Master says. "He rips your virgin cunt apart."

At the thought of Master forcing my cunt and throat open on his massive erection, my orgasm punches through me, leaving me writhing and gasping.

"That's right," he murmurs, and I know he's coming into her throat.

I ride out the aftershocks, shivering and twitching, and it's only when my mind starts to put itself back together again that I realize I forgot to use the dildo. I didn't even really touch myself much at the end. At some point I stilled my hand and just concentrated on what he was saying, let his mouth take me apart as surely as if he'd had it on me when I came.

Master sucks in a sharp breath through his teeth. "Don't disappoint me, Juliette," he commands.

Then he hangs up.

When my legs feel like they'll work again, I put the dildo away and start getting ready for bed. As I brush my teeth, wash my face, and put on my pajamas, Master's parting words ring in my ears.

I won't disappoint him. He assumed I used the dildo. I *can't*. I'm going to do this exactly the way he wants me to.

And so I'm going to let Jackson be my first.

7

I'VE JUST STEPPED out of the shower after a long, sweaty practice match when Jackson's name flashes across my phone. I'm the only person in the pristine white locker room. I tug my towel tighter before I hit *accept* on his call.

"Juliette," he says. "How did your homework go last night?"

"It was good," I say, flushing involuntarily at the memory of Master's voice coaxing me to orgasm. "But I didn't, um. I didn't end up using the dildo. I tried! I really did. But when I was thinking about it too much I locked up, the way I did with you. And then when I got really into it I just…forgot."

I take another paranoid look around the locker room. I would die if anyone here overheard me talking to my sex tutor about whether I could use my dildo last night. But the small palm trees in their terra-cotta planters are the only other living things in the room. I go to my locker, dropping my towel and putting him on speaker so that I can get dressed as we talk.

"It was useful, though," I assure him. "I learned a lot. It's going to be fine. I'm looking forward to seeing you later."

"I'm glad to hear that," he says. I shimmy into my panties and a pair of shorts. "But Juliette, I'm a patient man. I know you want to please me, but I won't enter you until I really believe that you want me to fuck you. You've spent a long time thinking of your virginity as an asset, and it's natural that you'd need some time to adjust to the idea that it really isn't."

"I understand that." I slip my shirt over my head, grab my gym bag and head out of the locker room, so I can continue this conversation somewhere more private. The idea of getting caught turns me on, but I don't want to get caught. I can't help picturing Susan's shocked face in the sauna at Les Bains.

"I'm sure I can do it," I tell Jackson. "Want to meet at your house later? I'll prove it to you." I won both of the sets I played against Layla today, and the victory is still sweet in my mouth; I feel confident in this moment that everything's going to go exactly the way I want it to.

"I can do that," Jackson says. "Tell me, though: how would you like it? How should I prepare? I can be anything you want. If you tell me what that is."

I glance around the lobby, which is just as deserted as the locker room was. Still, I'm almost whispering when I ask, "Can you talk dirty?"

"What kind of dirty?"

There's another stand of potted palms in the lobby, and I duck behind a corner one.

"Can you tell me to get on my pretty knees and suck you like a whore?"

The knowledge that anyone could overhear me adds a zing down my spine and between my legs. My body is tired but I'm happy, and I like imagining lying down on Jackson's bed and letting him fuck me, the windows in his big beautiful house wide open so anyone can see. Like Jane wants, I will be the doll on the pedestal. I imagine going to Master's office and telling him that I did it, I did everything that he needed me to do, just like I always do and always will.

"And when I'm sucking your cock, can you say I have a pretty mouth?"

"I can do all that," Jackson promises. I imagine him saying these words with his mouth against my neck, pressed into my sternum, or the inside of my thigh, and shiver helplessly. "I'll see you this afternoon."

He hangs up, and I take a long, deep breath before I turn around...to find Vaughn Devonshire right behind me, as rakish and handsome as he was the first time he caught me doing something naughty. I wonder how much of that he heard—I was explicit enough that there's no mistaking what I was talking about.

Strangely, though, I don't mind the idea. I'm promised to someone who isn't Vaughn, who wants me to be on the phone with strange men, practicing my dirty talk. What Vaughn—or anyone else—thinks of that doesn't really matter.

He draws closer to me, so that we're both half-sheltered behind the palm's fronds, and no one passing by can see that he's leaning in as if he's about to kiss me. "It's nice to run into a friendly face again," he murmurs. "I've just moved stateside after some years overseas, so I don't know many. Even fewer as beautiful as yours is."

"Where overseas?" I ask, trying to keep it light, even though I know he can see that my nipples are stiff, and my breath is coming a little too fast. Between the conversation I was just having with Jackson, and Vaughn's closeness, the scent of him surrounding me and the heat of his body radiating through his clothes, I feel almost light-headed with desire. I'm just proud of myself for being able to form a coherent question.

He smiles, and doesn't answer. "Would you like to meet me for coffee?" he asks.

I would. "Sure," I say. "But I should tell you, I'm contracted to marry already."

His mouth is centimeters from my neck, an aching tease, when he says, "Oh, I know."

"You do?"

"He's been waiting a long time."

So Vaughn knows who *he* is. Would he tell me?

Probably not, but he knows exactly how to get me hot, and if he knows my husband, he might also know that he doesn't care about my virginity. So what's one coffee? What's the point of having all this time and freedom if I don't take advantage of it?

"So, Juliette," Vaughn says, and I tilt my head back, baring my throat to him, begging him to close the gap between us. He doesn't, though. He steps back and asks, "What do you say?"

"I say...maybe," I tell him, and brush past him, through the lobby and out the front doors, my panties damp but—on the whole—pretty pleased with myself.

8

My GOOD MOOD lasts all the way home. I walk up the front lawn and around the main house, down the path home, pausing briefly to finger the velvet petals of the late-summer roses that are lifting their faces to the sun. When I look up, I see Jane walking out of the main house, and pause to wait for her so we can walk together.

"How was the tennis club?" she asks after a kiss on the cheek.

"I beat Layla twice. But even better—I ran into Daddy's friend Vaughn. The one who came over for dinner the other night? He asked me out."

Jane gasps with delight. "What did you say?"

"I told him the truth—that I was already contracted. But I guess he knows, and doesn't care, so we're going to meet up."

"Are you excited?"

"I am," I say. "He's so gorgeous, Jane—his eyes are this crazy light blue, and the way he smiles at me... He just *looks* like sex. And his smell—you know how some men have that clean, spicy smell that just drives you crazy?"

Jane pushes the front door open, and I follow her inside. "What are you going to do with him?" she asks as we walk into my bedroom. The answer is, I don't know. The answer is, I haven't filled out my Vaughn fantasy.

But I don't have a chance to ask for advice, because there are two men in my room.

One of them is Jackson, wearing his customary loose, light linen, but he's with another man who I don't recognize. The second guy is younger than Jackson—closer to my age, probably. He looks like Jackson picked him up off the beach. His hair is sun bleached and his tan is deep and even. He has a surfer's long, muscular arms, and dark eyes.

"Jackson," I blurt out. "I didn't know—is everything okay?"

"Everything is fine," he assures me. "Master didn't tell you I was coming?"

"You called him?" I don't know why this terrifies me when it's obvious I'm not in trouble. Yet.

"Juliette, this is Nathan."

I shake his hand automatically. Nathan is insanely good-looking, with the kind of face that would have made me swoon when I was just a little bit younger. He doesn't exactly do it for me, though, and I don't know why.

"Nice to meet you," I say. "Nathan, Jackson, this is my... friend, Jane."

"Nice to meet you," Jane echoes faintly. I look at her and see that she's eyeing Nathan with raw animal lust.

"I've been thinking," Jackson says. "That when we tried to fuck before, maybe it was the scenery making you uncomfortable. Or maybe you're resistant to me, as a man, which is fine. So I thought we might try it here, and if that doesn't work, I brought Nathan, in case he's more to your tastes."

He isn't. He's beautiful, but he's not for me. In this

moment, I'm not sure either of them is. That anyone is, aside from Master and hopefully, my husband. Presented with this reality, I'm not ready at all.

From beside me, Jane says, "I should go."

Before I have time to think, I'm telling her, "No. Stay."

She looks at me, a question in her eyes, and I can only shrug in response. But I can't stop thinking about how Jane told me a few weeks ago that she wished that she was being trained—that someone would teach her the skills I was learning, so she'd be more certain of herself in the bedroom. I can't give her that, of course, but can I include her in this lesson in some way? I'd like that, especially if it means she gets to touch Nathan. She so clearly wants to, and from the way he's looking at her, I think he wouldn't mind.

Is that crazy? I wonder. Susan would probably choke on her tongue if I described this to her, asking my companion to fuck my sex tutor so I could watch and learn, and keep my pussy to myself. But Susan wouldn't understand anything I've done so far, and I've enjoyed a lot of it. Plus, I know all about how she fantasizes about being watched—put on display like a doll.

Every aspect of this is something she wants. And something I can give her.

If it gets me out of something I *don't* necessarily want to do, that's just an added bonus.

"Jane," I say. "You want more experience with men, don't you?"

She nods.

"Do you—would you want to fuck Nathan?"

She nods, her cheeks as cherry-red as if she'd been slapped.

"Would you mind if I watched?"

She shakes her head.

I turn to Jackson. "That's what I'd like then," I say. "For Jane and Nathan to have sex, and I can watch and learn."

Jackson considers it. "I can work with that," he says at last.

Jane can't keep the smile off her face. She throws her arms around me and presses her face into my neck. "Thank you," she whispers. "Oh my God, Juliette, this is incredible."

"Enjoy it," I say, giving her a little squeeze before we separate.

"Okay," Jackson said, his voice still calm and even, but slipping into that authoritative mode that gets me going every time. "Both of you, take off your clothes."

We undress quickly; I'm glad that I showered before I came home, and a little ashamed that I'm not wearing sexier lingerie. But then, no one warned me this was going to happen. And anyway, it doesn't matter, since I'm out of it before anyone's really had time to look.

"Lie down on the bed for me, Jane, and spread your legs," Jackson says.

Jane does. She's already wet, and she shivers when he palms at her pussy, rubbing his fingers gently along her seam. "She's already turned on, which is nice," Jackson says to me. "That means something is working—that there's an attraction here, and that her body and her mind are on the same page. So now I'm just going to help her along a little bit. Give her some friction, some fullness." He circles her clit carefully with his thumb. "Gorgeous," he murmurs.

I watch as gooseflesh breaks out on Jane's skin.

"Now," he says to me, "I want you to put your mouth here and suck her. Feel what it feels like when I have you on my tongue."

"No," I say. "I'm not doing that." I love Jane, but I'm not ready to go there with her yet. Or ever, probably. "That's a line I'm not ready to cross."

I expect Jackson to argue with me, but instead he says, "Tell Nathan how to do it, then, in your place."

I take a deep breath, then turn to Nathan and gesture for him to kneel between Jane's legs, which he does. I watch as he kisses her spread thighs. I think about what turns me on, where her fantasies and mine intersect.

"Open her up," I tell him, and he does. "Show us how soft and pink she is." He parts her folds and displays her glistening pussy to us. She lets her knees fall further to the sides, eager to show us more.

"She's a good girl, isn't she?" I ask. Like Master would. "She deserves a reward for being so good. Dip your tongue inside of her. In and out, slowly." She's quivering with want as he obeys me, fucking her ever so slowly with his flattened tongue, still holding her open to the air and our eyes. I like the slow anticipation of the tease, but more than that, I like to be at the mercy of a man who knows just what to say and do and touch and lick, so I give my friend the same relief.

"Her clit needs your full attention now, Nathan."

He takes his time teasing her, licking up and around, before he gets his lips around her clit. When he does, Jane stuffs her fingers in her mouth to keep from crying out.

"Now you," Jackson says to me. "Get on your pretty little knees."

I do, watching as he pulls his cock out and strokes himself hard. "Open that pretty mouth for me," he commands, and I do that, too, but even though he's saying the words—they just don't sound right. He's giving me my fantasy—but my heart's not in it.

I gave Antoine so many blow jobs that I can throat Jackson without even thinking about it, letting him fuck my mouth at a leisurely pace. He threads his fingers through my hair and pulls me forward and then back again, but the little shock of pain to my scalp doesn't sizzle down my spine, doesn't lick at my clit. It just feels like a reminder that even though I'm doing exactly what I'm supposed to be doing, and he's saying exactly what I asked him to say, my mind isn't here.

It's with someone else, someone it shouldn't be with, and I won't let myself think of him.

"Okay," Jackson says at last, with a sharp tug of my hair. "Up."

I stand.

Nathan is standing, too; Jane is still lying on the bed, staring at the ceiling in a daze. "I'm going to fuck you now," he tells her. "You want that?"

"Yes," she says, and her voice is full of the edgy, aching want that I've been trying and failing to summon.

"Let her ride you," Jackson instructs. "I want Juliette to be able to watch."

Nathan lies down on the bed. He's hard already, cock standing proud against the smooth, taut skin of his stomach. Jane swings a leg over his hips so that she's sitting with her back to him; he palms her ass appreciatively before giving it a gentle *smack*. Then he reaches down and guides his cock to rub against her where she's wet.

"Please," Jane says. "Please give it to me. Fuck, please—" And Nathan doesn't make her wait any longer. He puts a hand on her hip and guides her as she sinks down onto him, his length disappearing inside of her body.

"Stay there for a minute," Jackson says. "Does that feel good, Jane? Having something inside of you?"

"He's so big," she says. "Oh. Oh. It feels so good."

"You can start to move when you're ready," Jackson says. "Fuck yourself on his cock."

He's been standing behind me a little ways away; now he

draws in closer, close enough that I can feel his breath on my neck, just where Vaughn was driving me crazy yesterday. He puts one hand on my belly and with the other starts to play with my nipples, pinching and stroking them until they're pink and puffy.

"I like this position because it gives the woman some control," Jackson mouths against my ear. "You see how she can set the pace?"

I nod.

"You should play with your clit while you watch," Jackson says. "You can play with yours too, if you want, Jane. Nathan, spank her again. I think she liked it the first time."

I get my hand between my legs and find I'm not as wet as I'd expect to be; perhaps because I'm not completely present. I will my body to respond as it should. I can't fail today.

I match my rhythm to Jane who is working herself faster and faster with both her fingers and his cock, and when Nathan's second smack lands on her ass, I moan along with her.

"See how much she likes it?" Jackson says to me. "Is your pretty little cunt ready to take me?"

"Yes," I tell him. I want this over with. I want it done so that I can start enjoying it like Jane does.

He pushes me forward so that I'm bent over the bed, braced on my arms, watching Nathan and Jane as their bodies move together. They look synchronized; she looks like she's getting exactly what she wants, being fucked full of hard cock while she rubs her clit and pinches her nipples.

Jackson parts my cheeks and presses his thumb against the skin there; I remember Master describing an anonymous man doing the same thing, and a ghostly shiver of desire washes over me. It vanishes just as quickly as it came, though, and by the time Jackson has slid his fingers down my seam, I'm tensed up again. He nudges against my cunt, trying to press inside, but I'm not wet enough and I'm not open, and there's just no way. He tries again and I can't bite back a yelp of pain. It doesn't sound like Jane did when Nathan smacked her ass for the first time. It sounds like someone who's genuinely uncomfortable and wants to leave.

I watch, helpless, as Nathan holds Jane's hips still and thrusts against her once, twice, three times before he comes, his orgasm finally triggering hers. She throws her head back and I'm caught by the expression on her face: her eyes closed and mouth open, face damp with sweat and pink with exertion. She looks so beautiful and so self-possessed, so completely and utterly blissed out.

After a long moment, Jane pulls herself off of Nathan, looking regretful that she has to move at all. "If you want the bathroom, it's just through here," Jane says, very shyly for someone who was coming on his cock just a few minutes ago. He follows her out of the room, leaving me and Jackson alone.

I stand up again, too ashamed to meet his gaze. "I'm sorry," I say.

"It's okay," he assures me. "It's not your fault. These things happen. Bodies are unpredictable."

For another few seconds, I let myself believe it's all going to work out.

Then he says, "However. I will have to call the agency and let them know that our lessons are running over schedule."

I sit down on the edge of the bed, shocked and numb and drained, as Jackson pulls out his phone and calls Master. My stomach curdles with fear.

"It's taking a little longer than expected," he says carefully. "And I was wondering what you thought the best move would be, given the circumstances."

Jackson nods at whatever Master is saying, his handsome face placid as he listens. He gives me a small smile. I can't return it. I am failing this lesson, no matter how safe and cared for I feel when he pats my thigh.

I know better than to trust his kindness. I know I am in danger of losing everything I've gained.

9

I WALK into Master's office the next day with my heart in my throat. He's concentrating on the papers in front of him on his desk; he doesn't even look up to greet me until he's finished paging through them, by which point, I've broken out in a cold sweat from head to toe.

"The eleven-p.m. phone call was bad enough," he says, slipping the papers into a folder that he pushes to the side of his desk. "But I don't want to get another phone call like the one yesterday, Juliette."

"Then don't give out your number," I say, in a weak attempt at humor.

Master doesn't acknowledge it. "Sit," he says, pointing to the armchair that's positioned opposite his plush couch. I sink into it, praying that this is the last time I'll disappoint him. Even though I know it won't be.

Master seats himself on the couch, and I keep my eyes fixed on the coffee table between us. It's completely bare—no magazines, no random files, not even an ornamental flower or plant. I think of Jackson's empty beach house, with its huge windows and blank walls, and wonder where Master lives, and what it's like there.

"Spread your knees apart," Master says, and so I do.

He doesn't seem pleased. "See?" he says. "Was that so hard? You were told what to do, and you did it. Why can't you just spread your legs for Palmer?"

Normally I would say something else snarky, or else clam up, but working with Jackson has gotten me used to talking honestly about my feelings, even when they're around something as personal and potentially shameful as sex. I picture his open, non-judgmental face as I tell Master, "I'm just not...turned on enough, I guess. I mean there's nothing wrong with him. He's sweet and super hot, and the foreplay is great, but the rest...it's just not...there." Then I start to worry that Master thinks I mean it's not there with me, instead of just between me and Jackson. "I'm not frigid or anything," I say, and my voice sounds strained even to my own ears. "I'm sure it'll be there for my husband."

"Juliette, I don't know where you got the idea that your virginity is some precious gem you can only give to one man, but it's holding you back." Master's gaze is unflinching, spotlight-bright. It makes me feel like he can see everything about me—everything. Just the weight of his eyes on me feels like it can pin me in place. "You're never going to finish here if you insist on prizing something my Client finds worthless."

"It's not worthless. It's just...special to me. Doesn't that make it worth something?"

"No."

I can't pretend that doesn't hurt my feelings, and he must be able to see it on my face. How can I marry a man who doesn't care about what I want? How can I expect that marriage might ever be a happy one?

Master's eyes flick down to my cunt, where I know he can

see the damp patch on my pale pink underwear. "When I told you to spread your legs, you got wet," he says.

I did, and knowing he's paying attention forces my pulse down between my legs. I'm flushed all over when I say, "So?"

"So you're capable."

Of course I'm *capable*. "Well, I mean, you got me off with *words* the other night."

He looks like a big cat all of a sudden, sleek and dangerous. "It's a gift," he intones, and his voice rumbles through me like thunder.

Then, in another instant, he's removed again, ice-cold Master a hundred thousand miles away. "Because I don't care how you feel or what you want," he continues. "And you don't have that gift, because you care too much."

"I know. You're right. I'll figure it out." I say the words, but I'm worried my promise is a lie.

Master shakes his head. "I've already figured it out," he says. "You've attached an importance to it that you refuse to get past. Get on the coffee table, faceup."

He stands, and I lie down, my feet on the floor and my hands laced over my stomach like maybe he's about to tell me to meditate or spank me for being so stubborn about this.

Instead, he spreads my legs and reaches under my skirt to tug my underwear halfway down my thighs. Before I have time to react, he's got his cock out and he's lining it up at my entrance. "You want it to mean something? You want it to be 'special'? So if I fucked you right now, got rid of your silly hymen so it wasn't such a distraction, you'd be disappointed because it wasn't boxed up in romance? Is that what I should do, Juliette? Just take it from you?"

He's big and hot, his tip poking just inside me, and I'm instantly drenched. He's testing me. I know this without a doubt and that the only correct answer to his question is silence, but I can't help myself. "Yes. Please."

I'm certain he won't do it, but there he is, pressing inside of me. There's no resistance, the way there has been with Jackson; he's huge, bigger than my fingers and bigger than the toy I was supposed to play with, but all I feel is ecstasy as he splits me open and fills me up.

He fucks me impersonally; he doesn't touch my clit or my breasts or anything aside from my deep inner walls. He doesn't even look at me more than he has to. He's silent the whole time.

But that doesn't matter. I've wanted this since the moment I laid eyes on him, and he doesn't have to do anything fancy to take me apart. His thrusts bury themselves deep inside my body, and I tighten around them just like I practiced; I can feel fragments of the time we've spent together in the air around us, as delicate and momentary as a spritz of perfume. I remember him teaching me how to spread my legs in this office and feeding me from his hand in a chic restaurant; I remember the private, intimate space of his car and the fantasy he whispered in my ear on the phone and just as I'm nearing the edge, he makes eye contact with me.

It's accidental, I think. He didn't mean to look at me, but once our gazes lock, he doesn't look away. His expression, still cold and stony, is subdued by the softness in his eyes.

"Ah, hummingbird," he whispers, the word flitting from him like it's been caged for too long, and I come undone, all of my internal muscles spasming on his cock. He lasts just a few moments longer and then he gives me one last brutal thrust, pulsing inside of me in hot wet spurts.

Then he pulls out, puts himself back in his pants, and takes a seat at his desk.

"Clean yourself up," he tells me, no trace of tenderness present, and I wonder if I imagined the moment. "You have 24 hours to finish with Palmer."

"Yes, Master."

I sit up, rearranging my skirts around myself, smoothing down my hair. I'm not a virgin anymore. I always knew I'd never forget Master, but now he's a part of me forever; when I think of my first, I won't think of my husband's face or the sheets of my marriage bed. I'll think of the ceiling of Master's office, and the sound of his belt buckle, and how all it took was him inside of me and his pet name for me on his lips to bring me to shaking, shuddering orgasm.

Master presses the intercom button on his phone. "Is my ten-twenty-two here?" he asks.

I collect my bag and head towards the door as his secretary pipes back, "Yes, sir."

"Juliette."

I turn back to him, hoping for…something. A "*good girl.*" A piece of advice. Anything to make me feel less like I'm still balanced on the knife's edge, uncertain about what matters anymore, who I am and what I want.

Instead, he says, "No excuses and no more complaints." Then, to his intercom, he says, "Send her in."

10

THE WHOLE CAR RIDE HOME, my head spins and spins. I can still feel the phantom of Master between my legs, the thickness of his cock as he pressed inside of me, the heat of his body next to mine. I'm not a virgin. He swears it doesn't matter to my husband. He says if it doesn't matter to my husband, it shouldn't matter to me. He tried to make it not matter to me, and instead, by taking me himself, he's made it matter more.

And yet it's very clear, it doesn't matter to him.

I feel unsettled and anxious all the same.

To make things worse, Jane misinterprets my blue mood. She finds me in the kitchen, listlessly fixing myself a cup of tea, and immediately starts apologizing. "I'm so sorry about the other day," she says. "I got caught up in my fantasy, but I never should have just fucked Nathan and given anyone the impression that you should have been ready to do the same. I can talk to Jackson if you want, apologize—"

"No," I assure her. "No, that's fine. I'm glad you had fun with him."

"Are you sure? Because—"

"I had sex with Master."

"Oh!" Jane's face lights up, and I know what she's imagining: something domineering and hot, him pushing me face-down on his desk and fucking me open on his cock, wringing orgasms out of me with his fingers and tongue. Nothing like what actually happened, which is that he was as impersonal with me as possible, and I came for him anyway, easy as anything.

"It's…complicated," I say.

Jane is still wearing her bathrobe; she toys with the tie on it. The kettle whistles, and she shoos me out of her way, setting out the strainer with my favorite loose-leaf jasmine tea, squeezing in a little lemon juice before she pours in the hot water. "Do you want to talk about it?"

I lean against the counter and let out a long sigh. "I had so many ideas about who my husband would be, and what I had to offer him," I say. "I thought I understood who I was supposed to be. But now I feel like I don't anymore, and what do I have? What am I worth to him now that I've been penetrated by someone else? It was already hard enough not to think about him. He's been in my head for months. It's almost—I'm almost starting to hate him." I don't tell her how I'm starting to feel about Master.

Jane picks up my tea and together we walk into the living room. I settle onto the couch, and she sits next to me, the warmth of her nearness a familiar comfort. "I think it might be a good thing," she says. "You needed to lose it one way or the other, and it wasn't going to happen with Jackson, or Nathan, or anyone else, probably. You needed to have sex, and now you have. It's just sex. And now it's done."

I sip my tea and try to look like I agree with her, but my face must give me away, because she shifts so that she's facing me and says, "Or, okay, think of it this way. What does this husband have to offer you? What's he worth, now that you've let another man come inside of you? You're starting to know what kind of sex you want, and like. He won't be your one and only. So he'll have to be good, because you'll know the difference."

That's...interesting.

"Maybe," Jane says, warming up to her subject now, her green eyes glowing with excitement, "he's so good he *knows* that nothing you do in training will measure up. Imagine that!"

I can't imagine anyone being better than Master, or maybe I just don't want to. But still, Jane's right: that's something to think about. A man confident enough in his skills that he doesn't care who comes before him, because he knows he'll obliterate the memories of them.

The idea shivers through me, hot and delicious.

"In that case," I say, leaning back against the couch. Its soft cushions embrace me like a gentle hug. "Maybe I should really be sowing my oats right now. Experiencing everything I can, so that I have plenty to compare him to. So I can see if he's really as good as he thinks he is."

Jane smiles at me. "I think that's a perfect plan," she says.

11

THE FIFTH HOLE of the Hillside Country Club's golf course is one of my favorites: it's right in the middle of the property, so it's surrounded on all sides by acres of quiet green, so serene that sometimes I fudge my putts a little bit just so we can stay longer.

Today, though, I'm not thinking about the shade of the massive oak trees nearby, or the clear blue water in the pond that's just over the next hill. Instead, all of my attention is focused on arguing with Daddy.

"What if I don't go through with it?" I ask him. "What if I just say no? Not because I'm quitting, but maybe the whole experience made me change my mind about like...my life?" I haven't been able to get my conversation with Jane out of my head since we talked the other day. What does my husband have to offer me, if our values are apparently so different? Am I not allowed to decide that one of these men suits me better than he does?

Daddy has been waiting for me to take my shot for long enough, so I nudge my ball a few feet and step aside to let him take his turn.

"You're not getting a better offer," he tells me.

"Well, maybe I should be the one making offers."

He ignores me in favor of turning to his caddy to change out his club. We've been having this argument since we teed off, and apparently he's decided he's done now. This is how fighting with him always goes—when he decides he's not interested anymore, he just stops speaking to me until I change the subject.

Well, I'm not in the mood today. I wave my caddy off and stomp back up to the clubhouse. My father can finish the course or not—I'm done pandering to him when he won't even listen to me about what I want for my life.

When I walk through the doors, the air-conditioned air is a welcome relief after standing in the sun all morning. I pause there for a moment, trying to re-orient myself, and figure out what I want to do next.

When I open them, Vaughn is standing in front of me. I would mind how he always appears out of nowhere if he didn't make my heart jump with a thrill every time he does it. He's wearing slacks and a polo shirt; where it's open at the throat I can see a hint of his chest hair peeking out. His forearms are well-muscled, and the pants fit painfully well.

He doesn't seem surprised to see me. Instead, he offers me his arm. "I guess you took me up on my offer for coffee," he says.

I take it, appreciating the feeling of his warm skin against mine. "I guess I did," I say. I'm ready to follow him anywhere —to the clubhouse's restaurant or a coffee shop in town, or straight to his bedroom, where he can lay me out and fuck me until we're both exhausted.

Instead, Daddy comes striding in through the doors, holding out his phone to me.

I know before I take it that it's Master on the line.

"What are you doing right now?" he asks.

Well, he wanted me to loosen up and not treat my body like it was anything too special, so he should be pleased to hear this news, I think. I smile up at Vaughn and say, "I'm meeting up with this guy my dad knows."

"Over my dead body."

I've never heard him sound this agitated before—even when he was angry with me, it was always at a cool remove, disappointed, not mad. Now, though, he sounds like a storm gathering, big, black clouds on the horizon.

Well, let him storm if he wants to. I'm done taking commands from him. I walk a few steps away and pitch my voice low. "But you said sex means nothing," I remind him. "So if sex means nothing, why can't I fuck who I want?"

"You are not a free agent," he growls. "You fuck who I say, how I say, when I say, until the Client—your husband—takes on those responsibilities."

But that sounds like a bad deal to me. I've had a taste of freedom, and liked it; I'm tired of being controlled. I get to decide what I want to do with my body and my time and my life. I want what matters to me to be important. I'm already walking back towards Vaughn when I say, "Fuck off," to my Master, each word clear and crisp. And then I hang up the phone.

Vaughn is looking at me with surprise and interest, a smile quirking the corner of his handsome mouth. Daddy is behind me, furious and shocked. And I—what *do* I want? Do I want to obey Master, like I have so far? I barely know Vaughn; sure, I want to fuck him, but it doesn't go beyond that, and if I leave with him, I'm blowing up my entire future.

Do I want pleasure in the moment? Do I want this man I barely know? Or do I want Master, who's been difficult and distant, but who has always taken care of me when I needed it?

No, I realize. I don't want any of that. I can't think about it in terms of Vaughn or Master. I have to think about myself.

And what I want more than anything is to finish what I started. Not because Master or the Client or my father said to. But because this is my experience, and I'm going to have as much of it as I can.

I hand the phone back to Daddy, kiss Vaughn's cheek in a gentle goodbye, and go out to get my driver to take me where I need to go.

12

———

JACKSON'S DOOR swings open almost as soon as I've knocked on it, as if he's been waiting for me. Did Master tell him to expect me? How did he know my decision before I'd even made it?

It doesn't matter. Jackson's face lights up with a smile when he sees me, and for once, the sight of him goes straight to my groin. I'm ready to tangle my fingers in his sandy hair, to kiss the line of his neck and let his strong, capable hands spread my legs and slip between my folds. I don't say anything, and even the silence between us feels electric.

"Come in," he says. He leads me to a room I haven't been in before—it's on the second floor, with more windows over-looking the bay below us. The décor is still simple, but less impersonal than it was downstairs. The walls are painted a gorgeous sky blue, and both bedside tables hold vases almost overflowing with jasmine. The scent of them is sweet and ripe in the air, mingling with the brine that blows in from the sea, and I know that every time I smell jasmine from now on, I'll remember Jackson and this house and this afternoon.

"I have to make a quick phone call," he says. "Do you mind waiting?"

I shake my head. He leaves the room, and once I'm alone, I strip my clothes off: I had fantasized about being unwrapped like a package, but my golf outfit wasn't very sexy, and I don't want to be thinking about it when he comes back. I'm ready to take what I want, and right now, what I want is Jackson.

When he returns, he's carrying two glasses of white wine. I'm sitting at the edge of the bed, my body on display, and I feel his gaze on me as I stand to take one from him. "You look gorgeous," he murmurs. "A man couldn't want much else."

I clink the edge of my glass against his and take a sip. The taste floods me with memory: it's the same wine he served the first day we met. He said then that it seemed right for our first session, and I'm glad he remembered it for our first time in bed together.

But I didn't come here to do a tasting, so once I've swallowed, I set the glass down on the bedside table and turn to face him. "How do you want me?" I ask.

His mouth curls into a wicked smile. "Come here," he says. Jackson pulls me close, pressing my naked body against his clothed one, and it feels deliciously filthy to rub my nipples against the stiff linen of his shirt, to feel the texture of his cotton pants on my bare pussy as he shoves his thigh between mine. He kisses me deeply, passionately; he plunders my mouth just as expertly as I know he's going to plunder my pussy.

His hands cup my shoulders and take a torturously slow path down my body, tracing the curves of my spine and my hips, finally coming around to rest on my ass. I can feel where he's hard against me, and I want to taste him—to give him some of the same pleasure he's giving me.

I drop to my knees and smile up at him, hoping I look as seductive as he did a few moments ago. Jackson pets my head while I get his pants open and pull out his cock.

I'm grateful for all the practice I had with Antoine: I can slide him down my throat with almost no resistance, sucking him down until he's sheathed in my mouth, and all I can taste anymore is him. "Good girl," Jackson says. "Fuck, look at how you take it. Are you wet for me, Juliette?"

I hum my *yes*.

"I want you to touch yourself while you suck me," he says. "Make sure you're slick and open so I can fuck your pussy the way I'm fucking your mouth."

I moan as he pulls out and then thrusts in again, not the brutal, careless way that Antoine took me, but with luxurious indulgence, like he just can't get enough of the plush heat of my throat. My fingers dip between my legs and I'm already soaking wet for him. I let him set the pace, fucking myself on my hand while he uses my mouth.

"I could come like this," he tells me. "I bet you could, too. But that's not what we're doing today, is it, Juliette? Take my cock out of your mouth and go lie down on the bed."

I do. The sheets feel like heaven beneath me: the thread count is high enough to feel like clouds, soft even on my over-sensitized skin. I spread my legs without being asked, and Jackson looks down at my cunt with hungry eyes. He gets on the bed with me, kneeling between my thighs, and kisses me again, tasting his own salt on my tongue.

His cock is bobbing between us, rock hard and slick with my spit, and I can't remember why I didn't think I wanted it; it would be so easy to just reach down between us and pull him inside of me, let him split me open the way Master did in his office the other day. I make myself wait, though. I don't want to rush this. I don't want to try to take over Jackson's plans.

"I've been waiting so patiently to taste your cunt again," Jackson tells me. "You were so sweet for me last time. Will you let me lick you again, Juliette?"

I want that very badly, but I'm already wound tightly; every time Jackson touches me, I feel like sparklers are going off under my skin. "I want that, but I'm afraid I'll come," I tell him, helplessly honest.

"Why would you be afraid of that?" he asks. "I want you to feel good all over, as many times as you can." He palms my pussy and smiles. "You're so wet for me," he says. "Do you think you can come twice? Once on my face and once on my cock?"

I'm not sure I can, but I want to. And I am nothing if not an excellent student, so I give him a playful little push on his shoulders. He gets the message.

Jackson kisses his way down my body: he plays with my nipples, licking them until they're just as stiff and wet as my clit, and tugs at them with his teeth. He kisses my navel and my hipbones, between my thighs. I'm shaking by the time he finally licks a long, firm strip up my cunt, the point of his tongue teasing at my clit. I throw my head back and moan.

Then he really goes to work: he loops his arms under my legs and tugs my hips towards his face, lapping at my clit in a rhythm that already has my legs trembling with need. I'm curled in on myself, watching this gorgeous man fuck me with his tongue, the muscles in his back shifting as he eats me out.

Just before my orgasm undoes me, I catch a glimpse of myself in the mirror on the far wall. Everything in here is lit by the same golden mid-afternoon light, but my reflection is sort of strange and dim, almost like the mirror is a two way. Like someone's on the other side, watching me watch myself.

Is it possible? Who could it be? Memories of Vaughn in my bathroom wash over me, combined with the idea of

Master, the fantasy of my husband. It doesn't matter. Whoever he is, let him look. Jackson tugs on my clit ring, gives me that little zing of pain that turns my world inside out and tumbles me over the edge, and I'm coming, shaking out of my skin as I pant and gasp.

When I come back to myself, Jackson is kissing my neck, and his cock is nudging at my entrance. "That was perfect," he tells me. "You ready to get fucked now?"

I'm past the point of words. I lift my hips up and let him fuck into me, my hands clawing at his shoulders as I try to urge him deeper and deeper. "Look at you, wildcat," Jackson says. "You were made for this."

The scent of jasmine mixes with the musk of our bodies; I reach up and wrap my hands around the bars of the bed's frame, arching my back so that whoever's watching can see the curve of my back and how my tits bounce every time Jackson thrusts into me. How eager I am, how supple, how ripe for the taking. Maybe there's no one there and I'm imagining the whole thing, but it doesn't matter: it's what I want, and so I give it to myself. Jackson fucks me until we're both coming, his cock spurting deep and wet inside me as I spasm around him, and my mind and my body have never felt so in sync.

13

THIS TIME, Master is waiting for me in the conference room where we first met. That day I was overwhelmed by the details of the room, but now I barely notice them as I throw the door closed behind me and announce, "Now that I realize I have options, I don't want your Client anymore."

Master doesn't even pretend to take me seriously. He just laughs and leans back in his chair. "You're bought and paid for," he says.

"What?"

There's a silence while he doesn't even attempt to explain himself. And I know what he means—my father promised me to this man when I was born, practically, and he's paid for my expensive training here with Master, but we could pay him back if we needed to. It's not like my family doesn't have money of our own.

"Well, maybe I won't like HIM now that I've had others," I try.

"How would other men change your opinion of a man you've never met?"

I give Master my most challenging glare. I'm tired of

being kept in the dark. I've done everything they asked of me. Now I want some answers. "What's he got that's worthwhile?"

Master sighs. "Juliette, these matches aren't random," he tells me. "You're not just given to any man who can pay for you."

Okay, *that's* news to me. I'm not?

"You've been tested since you were very young, and there are things you don't know about yourself yet. All of them play into which men you were offered to, and which ones wanted you. Your match, I have to say, is one of the most perfect I've ever made."

I should be thrilled to hear that phrase—*the most perfect I've ever made*. All I want is to know that in the end, all of this will have been worth it.

Instead, I say, "What, exactly, don't I know about myself?"

"We'll talk about it tomorrow," he says. "Here are your instructions for what to wear to our appointment."

Master Class continues with Lesson Four Submit

I'm determined to make M proud.
To earn the pearls he gave me.
He left me three boxes.
One for each test I'll have to pass.
Except I can't study for these.
All I have to do is everything they say…

Get Submit

ALSO BY RAVEN JAYNE

MASTER CLASS

A collection of dirty, erotic novellas

Lesson One: Obey

Lesson Two: Tempt

Lesson Three: Take

Master Class: First Three Lessons

Lesson Four: Submit

Lesson Five: Offer

Lesson Six: Play

Lesson Seven: Trust

Lesson Eight: Break

Lesson Nine: Master

Lesson Ten: Choose

PAIGE PRESS

Paige Press isn't just Laurelin Paige anymore...

Laurelin Paige has expanded her publishing company to bring readers even more hot romances.

Sign up for our newsletter to get the latest news about our releases and receive a free book from one of our amazing authors:

Stella Gray
CD Reiss
Jenna Scott
Raven Jayne
JD Hawkins
Poppy Dunne

ABOUT THE AUTHOR

Two NYT erotica authors got together and thought up a dirty little story. You're welcome.